THE
Husband
MAKER

THE *Husband* MAKER

KAREY WHITE

Orange Door Press

ISBN: 978-1-941898-03-1

Published by Orange Door Press

Other Books by Karey White

Gifted

For What It's Worth

My Own Mr. Darcy

Maggie's Song
(From the Timeless Romance Anthology: Love Letters
Collection)

Lost and Found
(A Ripple Effect Romance Novella)

For that girl I knew in college,
the one who was a husband maker
(you know who you are)

I'm glad you never gave up.

Chapter 1

I'd always heard the view from Top of the Mark was exceptional. When San Francisco Life listed the top ten places to view the skyline at night, Top of the Mark was ranked number three, so when the invitation to Harrison's wedding arrived, I finally had an excuse to take in the view for myself.

Stupid, stupid me. I should have taken a cab up the steep hills to 999 California Street, hopped on the elevator to the nineteenth floor, and looked out the windows. I could have come with or without makeup, and I could have worn jeans and a t-shirt. If I'd brought Mia or Aleena with me, we could have had a nice dinner or dessert. If I'd brought Angus, we could have had both. Since Top of the Mark was built at the crest of Nob Hill, I could have snapped a jaw-dropping photo or two with my iPhone and made the sparkling skyline my screen saver.

But no. I had to come see it on the night my old boyfriend was marrying a 49ers cheerleader named Nicki, who'd had more remodeling than an episode of *Property Brothers*. She looked like a Who's Who of Hollywood parts—

Scarlett's nose, Angelina's lips, and Kim's cheekbones. Her bias-cut dress clung to her other (ahem) purchased body parts and made me feel very un-girly in comparison.

"Nicki, this is Charlotte." Harrison looked me level in the eye, and for the first time all evening, I felt an inch of relief that things hadn't worked out between us. Five-eleven is pretty average for a guy, and Harrison towered over Nicki, even in her stilettos. But the only way he'd ever have been able to look down at me the way he'd looked down at Nicki when they'd exchanged their vows was if he'd stood on a stool. I know it's not important, and it makes me sound completely shallow, but I read a romance once where the leading man "gazed down at his true love with tender eyes." Someday, I'd like a guy to gaze down at me with tender eyes. And I'd rather not have to be standing in a hole for that to happen.

"It's fabulous to finally meet you." Nicki's voice was chirpy, and her lips didn't move quite right. "I want to thank you for breaking his heart"—she puckered up and baby-talked—"so I could put it back together." She pulled him down by his tuxedo lapel to kiss his cheek, then wiped the red smear away with her acrylic-nailed thumb.

Well, this was awkward. And I wasn't the only one feeling it. Harrison's eyes begged me not to set the record straight.

You see, Harrison had broken up with me. "I'm not ready for the whole settling down with one woman thing," he'd said four short months ago. "You're ready to get married, and I won't be ready for that scene for years."

Maybe he'd meant dog years.

"Congratulations, you two. You make a much better couple than we ever did," I said, although it stung to admit it.

"Did Will come? I saw Angus a little while ago,"

Harrison said. Will is my twin brother. No, his name is not Wilbur, although we've been asked if our1 parents had a thing for *Charlotte's Web* more times than I can count. His name is William, and he's the reason I ended up dating Harrison in the first place.

Our families lived on the same street in Fairfield, but I barely remembered Harrison, who was two years older than us. Nearly a year ago, Will and Harrison had been at the same concert, and Harrison had asked Will if his little sister was still available. Will wasn't sure if he meant me or McKayla, but since McKayla was already married, he gave Harrison my number. On our first date, Harrison admitted he hadn't been asking about me, but he was decent enough to say he was glad for the mix-up. And the rest is history.

A short and tragic history, but history nonetheless.

"Will and his wife are in D.C. right now interviewing." I stepped on my tiptoes and scanned the room over the groom's head. "I didn't know Angus was here."

"I talked to him earlier, but he might have left already," Harrison said.

"Aaahhh!"

I nearly knocked over a waiter as I jumped away from Nicki's scream. "Look, Kitten. It's Baxter Kensington. I didn't think he'd actually come."

Kitten? Did she really call him that? Harrison's red face confirmed that yes, she had. "He plays for the 49ers," he explained, and I nodded.

"I'd better go and make room for the celebrities," I said, and Harrison grinned. He'd always appreciated my sarcasm, and his cute grin jabbed at my not-quite-healed heart.

"Thanks for coming." He pulled me into a hug while his bride arranged her dress to best flatter her cleavage and patted the sides of her platinum fauxhawk. "Are things good with us?" he said quietly in my ear.

I pulled away. "Oh sure."

"I was worried—"

"Nothing to worry about. Go. Be happy."

"Thanks, Charlotte."

I turned away, my eyes stinging, and nearly barreled into one of the most stunning specimens of athleticism I'd ever seen. His pale yellow shirt and silvery gray suit contrasted beautifully with his dark skin. No wonder the bride was swooning about someone other than the groom. Poor Harrison looked like a little boy in comparison.

Ah, one of the hazards of marrying a cheerleader.

Through slightly blurred vision, I saw Harrison put his arm around Nicki. Not too long ago, I'd thought that would be me, though the venue and guest list would have been drastically different.

"Do you think he invited her?" A woman's voice echoed in the granite and chrome ladies' room.

"I don't know," another woman said. "Does the bride knows she's his old girlfriend?"

"She was more than a girlfriend. His mom thought he was going to marry her."

"Well, I did too. One day I was seeing Harrison and Charlotte at the movies, and the next I was getting a wedding announcement for Harrison and Nicki."

I'd made a little pit stop to wipe away my final Harrison tears. I was surprised I had any of those left to cry, but under the circumstances, I could allow myself a few. I'd been ready to step out of the stall, but now my feet were glued to the marble floor.

"That poor girl."

"The bride or Charlotte?" The women laughed, and I cringed. Why hadn't I just headed home?

"I meant Charlotte. I was shocked how quickly Harrison moved on."

I'd been a little shocked myself. I'd suspected he'd be engaged before too long, but the speed had surprised even me. How had he found a cure for his commitment phobia so quickly?

"Why do you think Charlotte has had such a hard time finding a husband? She's a beautiful girl. And so sweet. You know she was my Hannah's roommate at college." Now I recognized the voice. It was Mrs. Shelton.

"It must be hard to have your twin brother *and* your little sister both get married before you," the other woman said.

"Her sister could have afforded to wait a few years if you ask me. I wouldn't want my daughter to get married at twenty. I thought maybe she had to get married, but it's been a year and there's still no baby."

I wanted to speak up and defend McKayla. Connor was a wonderful guy, and they were happy. How was McKayla's wedding any business of these two old gossips?

"It's not surprising. McKayla was always gorgeous. She could have had anyone she wanted. Charlotte's not as flashy as McKayla, but she's still a pretty girl." I tried to get a peek at the woman who was speaking through the crack in the door, but I didn't have the right angle. All I could see was Mrs. Shelton applying cherry red lipstick.

"I think Charlotte's even prettier than McKayla, but that's just me." Thank you, Mrs. Shelton. The compliment made me a tiny bit less annoyed with her.

"Maybe she's too choosy. I think some girls get so picky

they won't give a regular guy a chance." Who was this knowledgeable woman?

"I don't think Charlotte is picky at all," Mrs. Shelton said, and I silently banged my head against the door of the stall. "Hannah said Charlotte dated lots of guys, but it never worked out. Maybe she's not picky enough. Whatever it is, somehow she just keeps driving guys away."

I'm too picky. I'm not picky enough. I'm beautiful, but I send guys running. This was exactly how I'd wanted to finish this evening. Maybe I'd get lucky, and these two women could gossip their way to a solution for my perpetual singleness. I could hardly wait to find out.

Now their voices got quieter, conspiratorial. "Hannah says they gave Charlotte a nickname in college. They called her 'the husband maker.'"

I gasped and quickly put my hand over my mouth.

The other woman laughed. "What does that even mean?"

"Well, Hannah said every guy Charlotte goes out with ends up marrying the very next girl he dates. The poor girl is jinxed."

"Oh, dear. Does she know they called her that? That could be hurtful."

No, I didn't know.

Of course I knew every guy went on to marry the next girl they dated, but I hadn't realized everyone around me had noticed the pattern. Who had called me that? Mrs. Shelton had said "they." How long had I been the butt of everyone's jokes? I remembered Hannah comforting me after a breakup. Had she just been trying to get information to share with others so they could have a good laugh at my expense?

"It may be cruel, but if it's true, you should set her up with Michael." I couldn't believe Mrs. Shelton was making jokes about me. She'd always been kind to my face. She'd even bought me a pink and gray comforter that matched Hannah's so our room could be color coordinated. And now she was laughing at me.

"It would be nice for Michael to get married and give me some grandchildren. My chances of being a cool, hip grandma are slipping away. But I don't think Charlotte's parents would approve of her dating someone who's forty-two," the woman said. "Although Charlotte's not getting any younger. Isn't she close to thirty?"

"I think she's the same age as Hannah," Mrs. Shelton said. "That would make her about twenty-six." I was actually twenty-five. For three more weeks, thank you very much. "I'm not saying she'd have to marry him. But if he dated Charlotte, he'd have it made. Even if he didn't end up marrying her, he'd marry the next girl he dated."

The women giggled like schoolgirls. "Hmm. That's not a bad idea. Michael could use a little . . ."

Their voices faded as they left the restroom. I collapsed onto the toilet seat and buried my face in my hands. I never wanted to face another person again. If I waited long enough, everyone I knew would leave, and I could sneak out, catch a plane to Honduras, and never look back.

If only I had a passport.

I'm not sure how long I sat there. Two people came in, used the restroom, then left. Pretty soon, my right leg started to go to sleep, and I knew I needed to move. And what was I doing sitting here? No matter how clean the bathroom looked, I'd been sitting on a public toilet. I was in worse shape than I'd thought.

I looked at my reflection with a critical eye as I washed my hands. My long hair was dark and shiny. My eyes were an interesting blue with specks of green and gold. I leaned toward the mirror and took inventory. I had good cheekbones and a good smile, thanks to three years of orthodontic care and nightly headgear worthy of a horror movie, and I had a little dimple at the left corner of my mouth.

"Someone could love me," I said to my reflection. When my reflection didn't answer, I left the restroom.

"Hey, Chuck, I'm glad you're still here." I was so glad to hear Angus's voice, even though I hated that nickname. "If I'd known you were coming, we could have come together."

I tried to speak, but a giant jawbreaker-sized lump had lodged itself in my throat, so I nodded.

"Harrison said you were here and . . ." His voice faded off. "Hey, are you okay?"

I bit my lips between my front teeth and nodded.

"You sure?" He put his arm around me, and my nod turned to a shake as he pulled me into his side. "Oh Chuck. Why do you do this to yourself?" I let him pull me into his arms and rub my back. "Do you need some therapy?" he asked softly, and I nodded into his shoulder. "Let's get out of here."

Luigi's sounds like it should have spaghetti and spumoni on the menu, but instead, it serves up the messiest barbecue ribs and the richest avalanche pie in the bay area. It's the perfect antidote for a broken heart because no one would ever choose to eat at Luigi's with someone they wanted to impress, so it would never be a date destination. It's impossible to eat the Carolina ribs while maintaining a level of decorum.

Years ago, after my first tragic breakup, Angus had

suggested we go get some ribs. The avalanche pie was my addition to our gastronomical therapy. Over the years, we'd "visited the therapist" whenever either of us had a breakup or experienced heartbreak. It almost made breakups a good thing.

Okay, that's overstating it, but I always feel a little better after we stuff ourselves.

Will thinks we're crazy, and he might be right. He came to this conclusion when we were in college. I'd been dating Skyler, a film major with a sensitive ponytail. He liked to eat Indian food and go to hole-in-the-wall theaters where we'd see artsy movies, or the plight of humanity portrayed in modern dance. Some of what we saw was great. Some might have made me stupider as I sat through them.

Skyler took off for some little town in North Dakota, or Saskatchewan, or some other bitter cold place to make a movie about a man who was braving the North Country without electricity. He hoped this would be his ticket to one of the smaller film festivals. He broke up with me from his cell phone in Montana. The coverage wasn't good, and his reception kept cutting out, so the whole breakup conversation took place over several hours and seven calls. To make a six-hundred-and-thirty mile story short, he explained he didn't want the baggage of a long-distance relationship distracting him from the job he was trying to do. It'd be best if we took a break until he came back four months later.

I agreed. I didn't want to be a distraction.

Skyler married a Cree woman named Amber Starblanket three months later. But my mind wanders.

After my lengthy phone call with Skyler, I called Angus to see if he was available for some therapy. According to Will, when Angus got off the phone, he fist-pumped the air and let out a whoop.

"You know she just broke up, right?" Will had asked.

"I know." Will told me Angus hadn't looked very sad for me.

"So why are you celebrating?"

"Oh. I don't know. I guess it's 'cause I'm hungry, and ribs sound good."

"You know you two can go eat ribs without Charles having her heart broken," Will had said. (Charles, Charlie, Chuck, even Chuckers—they used them all. Once, Will even called me Woodchuck. Sometimes brothers and their friends need to be smacked.)

"No, we can't. We've made a pact that we'll never eat at Luigi's except in an emergency."

"Well, at least try and show some sympathy."

"You know I will," Angus had assured him.

And he had. He always let me rant and rave and cry. He even let me have a bigger share of the pie if I wanted. And I'd done the same for him, although his dating history was much more sporadic than mine. Angus dated, but he was so focused on school that he had long dry spells between girlfriends.

I probably should have taken more breaks. Maybe then I'd have sent fewer men into the arms of matrimony. But there was something audaciously hopeful inside me. Or maybe it was fear. Whatever it was, I couldn't turn down a decent guy. What if I did and he was the one I was supposed to marry? What if I said no and the love of my life slipped through my fingers?

So I always said yes. And I always tried to make the best of every relationship because I wanted to find love. I wanted a wonderful husband and cute babies who would grow into chubby toddlers who would grow into awkward tweens and . . .

Well, you get the picture.

Anyway, I almost single-handedly kept Angus and me in therapy. Lucky for me, he was still single, or who would have joined me in our own little version of couples counseling?

Chapter 2

The valet looked skeptical when he climbed out of my car. Folding my five foot eleven inch frame into my classic Volkswagen Beetle was crazy enough. Watching Angus contort his way in was enough to give my spirit a little lift, and make the uniformed men at the curb shake their heads. When he was in the passenger seat, his knees near his ears and his always-a-little messy, sandy brown hair flattened against the roof, I pulled out onto California Avenue.

"I'm glad you took a taxi here, so we don't have to worry about two cars," I said.

"Easy for you to say. These cars weren't made for guys my size." Angus was almost six feet four inches.

"Technically, they probably weren't made for girls my size either, but at least I can park in my garage without scraping the sides." I'd purposely traded in my old sedan for this little car after Mia and I had moved into our tiny, two-bedroom walk up. It came with a garage that fit my car and our bikes. Mia refused to sell the SUV her parents had bought her for graduation, so she was stuck finding street parking—no easy task on a street filled with ground-floor businesses.

A light changed and a utility truck slammed on its brakes. I turned sharply to the left and pulled up beside it at the light.

Angus braced himself against the dashboard. "Easy, Chuck. Luigi's doesn't close 'til ten."

"When are you going to start calling me Charlotte? You and Will are the only Neanderthals who still use Chuck and Chuckers. They're hideous."

"Ouch. They're not hideous. They're cute, and we use them 'cause we love you."

"They're not cute. Especially in front of people."

"People like old boyfriends? Or cheerleaders?"

"Like anyone I've met in the last ten years." Was I fighting a hopeless battle?

Angus elbowed me. Not a hard thing to do in my clown car. "Charlotte sounds too mature and sophisticated. Like British royalty or something. Sorry, Charlie. I'm not sure I'll ever be able to call you Charlotte and take myself seriously."

"What about taking me seriously, Angus?"

"Maybe when we're grownups."

I blew out a raspberry sigh.

There was no winning this debate. We'd been through it way too many times. Will and I had been friends with Angus since first grade. For years, I'd been one of the boys—riding bikes, playing video games, and building forts. In elementary school, Dad started calling me Charlie. Soon it had been shortened to Chuck. In the fourth grade, I protested. It wasn't fair for me to be called a boy's name. Will didn't get called by a girl's name.

Dad remedied that by calling Will, Wilhelmina. That didn't go over so well, so after several months of protests, Dad reverted back to Charlotte and Will. But the damage had been done, and the guys continued to call me Chuck. I complained, but I'm pretty sure that made it worse. Finally I gave up.

"Can we sit toward the back?" Angus asked the hostess when we walked into Luigi's. The restaurant was nearly full, even though they closed in less than an hour. We sat down at a quiet booth in the corner.

Mrs. Shelton's words bounced around in my head. *They call her the husband maker.*

"That's quite a frown you've got going there."

"Sorry."

Angus dipped his head, forcing me to make eye contact with him. "Don't be sorry. Just talk to me."

"Have you heard anyone call me the husband maker?"

Angus leaned back in the booth and shook his head. His dark, worried eyes watched me. "Who told you about that?"

"So you have?" When he didn't immediately speak, I knew the answer. I sighed and leaned back against my seat as well.

There we sat, both of us slouching against our seats, looking at each other.

"Why didn't you tell me?" I whispered.

"Now why would I do that? Why would I purposely tell you something that would hurt your feelings?"

I should have appreciated his desire to spare me, but at the moment, I wasn't sure what to think. "Wouldn't a real friend be honest with me?"

"I was honest. If you'd ever asked me, I'd have told you. I wouldn't have lied to you. But I don't think a real friend would jump at the chance to share something hurtful. Wouldn't a real friend be protective?"

I shrugged.

"Who told you?"

"No one."

"Then how—?"

"I overheard Hannah Shelton's mom in the restroom. She was telling some other woman that everyone calls me the husband maker."

"Not everyone, Chuck."

"You know what I mean. And why shouldn't they? There I was at Harrison's wedding. I guess I just made him a husband. I guess I made Skyler a husband. And CJ and Jerry and . . . I can keep going if you want me to." I would have kept going to illustrate my point, but my voice was starting to quiver, and in a minute, I'd only have two options—cry or yell at Angus. As upset as I was that he'd never told me, I knew he didn't deserve to be yelled at. He was here for therapy, after all.

"Charlotte."

His voice was full of concern, and he used my given name, so I knew he wasn't kidding around.

"What?" My voice cracked.

He shook his head. "Don't worry about what people say. You've had bad luck. That's all. It isn't your fault."

The waitress brought out our food. "Can I get you anything else?"

"This is great, thanks." Angus wasted no time piling food on his plate. "I hope you're hungry," he said after she left.

"I can't believe we're eating this much food at almost ten."

"If the food doesn't take your mind off all this junk, the heartburn will."

I laughed.

Angus's voice turned serious again. "If you wish I'd have told you, I'm sorry I didn't."

I nodded. I wasn't sure I wanted the answer, but I had to

15

ask. "Have you ever called me that?"

"Of course not."

"Whew. Thanks." I gave him half a smile. "We may have to skip the pie tonight." I tucked a couple of napkins over my dress.

"Or get it to go." Angus piled food on his plate. "You know, Charlie is still single. I've thought several times I should set you up with him."

"Charlie and Charlie. It sounds ridiculous."

"His name is actually Charles. And he's a great guy." Charlie had been in one of Angus's study groups three years earlier. Angus swore up and down he was a great guy and that someday—when I was between boyfriends—he was going to play matchmaker. "He's taking a residency in Sacramento, so he won't be too far away. That's a date-able distance. Hey, if you dated him, I might have to call you Charlotte to keep you straight."

"Yeah, right. You'd call us Charlie and Chuck, and I'd still have the uglier nickname."

"I should give him a call."

"Thanks for thinking of me, but not now."

The ribs were exactly what I needed—sweet, tangy, and messy. We joked and laughed. I told Angus about the job I'd just finished—a tourist package for the Arkansas Alligator Farm and Petting Zoo. "They wanted a cartoon map, four post-cards, two key chains, and two refrigerator magnets."

"Did you go to Arkansas?" Angus asked.

"No. They didn't have a big enough budget for an on-site visit, so they emailed me all kinds of pictures. Not sure I needed to see the alligators in person anyway."

"I still can't believe this is a real job."

"Hey, it may not be as important as what an orthopedic surgeon does, but I work hard." Promotional materials and souvenir creation might sound like a made up profession, but I'd worked hard to get my position with Jayne Fife Graphics. When it had been Jayne, Patty and me, she'd called the position PMS (promotional materials and souvenirs) for short, but after she hired Brian and Keith, that acronym disappeared.

When I first started there, I mostly created menus and pamphlets, but after a while I'd become the go-to gal for all things touristy. Now I handled almost all the souvenir creation that came to Fife.

"I know you do. Maybe I'm jealous because you're out in the real world making decent money instead of getting ready to start a five-year residency."

"It'll be over before you know it."

"You've been saying that for eight years," Angus said pointing at my chin.

I dabbed with my napkin and laughed as I wiped away a glob of barbecue sauce. "Every time I say it, it's closer to being the truth. And at least now you'll be practicing medicine. That's gotta be pretty exciting."

"It is. I'll actually be in the operating room, and you're right, there's finally an end in sight."

"I'm so proud of you. You're going to be a great surgeon."

"I hope so."

"Do you know where you'll be doing your residency? Please say it's close by."

"I've narrowed it down to two options. Alameda County Medical Center has offered me a position. So has New York Methodist. I've done everything else here in the bay area. It might be nice to go somewhere new. See a new part of the country. New York would be interesting."

"New York's got nothing on Alameda." Angus had been

a part of our lives almost as long as I could remember. It would be hard to have him clear across the country.

Angus laughed. "I've got a few months to decide."

We were nearly sick so Angus ordered the pie to go. I put my fork down and rested my chin in my hand. Angus leaned back in his seat and sighed.

"You should take that home," I said. I was so full the pie the waitress brought didn't even look good.

"No, you should. This was your therapy session."

"I want you to take it. Share it with the guys."

"Nathan's on a no sugar kick, and Zach and I don't need a whole pie."

Angus motioned for the waitress. "Would it be possible to split this into two containers?"

"Sure." She took the pie, and Angus leaned forward. "Okay, be straight with me."

"Are we getting serious again?" I asked.

"Just for a minute." He took a deep breath. "Why do you do this to yourself?"

"Do what to myself?" I clasped my hands in my lap and braced for his answer.

"Come on, Chuck. You know what I'm talking about. Why do you go to these weddings? This has to be at least three that you've attended." It was actually four, but I wasn't going to admit that.

"I don't invite myself, you know."

"I know, but just because you get an invitation doesn't mean you have to go. Save yourself the heartache and stay away. Most of them don't deserve your time, and they certainly don't deserve a gift. What did you give Harrison?"

"A toaster."

"He didn't deserve a toilet plunger from you, Charlie. And he sure didn't deserve you standing there congratulating him and his new bride. You should have gone to the movies tonight or to the Warriors game."

"I can't afford a playoff game," I said.

"That's not the point. You should have done anything but put yourself through that."

"Perfect. Go ahead and criticize me for going. I dated him for long enough that we kinda became friends, you know. Why were you there? You guys hardly even know each other."

Angus quietly studied the salt and pepper shakers. "I was only there to be sure you were okay."

I gaped at him, but he didn't look up. "Oh." I wasn't sure what to say. "Sorry."

"Don't be sorry. You've got nothing to apologize for. I watch you making it easy for these guys who dump you—sorry, but most of them aren't nice—and I hate that you let them off the hook when I know most of the time you're still hurting."

"I'm not always hurting, Angus. Honestly, sometimes I don't even care that we break up."

"But it's happened enough that I know these weddings end up being a slap in the face. Even if you weren't in love with the guy. And I don't like you getting slapped in the face."

The waiter brought back the two boxes of pie and our check. We each left a few bills on the table and walked out into the twinkling night. The beetle was parked a block away, and at first we walked in silence. Finally, I couldn't stand the quiet any longer. I hugged Angus's arm. "Thank you for caring."

His burst of laughter startled me.

"I'm serious. I'm glad I have a friend who cares, but really, you don't have to worry about my heart."

"Tell you what, Charles. If you'll start worrying about it, I'll try to stop."

"Harrison got married?" Jayne shrieked and dropped into the chair across the desk from me. Jayne was all angles and no curves. She wore her dark hair short and would have looked like a teenage boy, except for the giant hoop earrings and bright red lipstick she wore every day. "I didn't even know you guys broke up. Why didn't you tell me?"

"I just did."

"Charlotte, if he's married, you broke up a long time ago."

"It's been a few months." I tried to act like it was no big deal.

"You're joking."

I shook my head. Jayne was looking at me like I'd sprouted antlers and had grown a beard of feathers.

"How is that possible? I thought you guys were kinda serious."

"Don't ask. I've quit analyzing my love life. It's too confusing."

Jayne closed her mouth and leaned forward in her chair. "Does this mean I can set you up with Kyle?" I buried my face in my hands. For the past year, she'd been trying to convince me that Kyle and I were perfect for each other. I'm not opposed to most setups, but Kyle was a different story. He was nine years older than me. NINE! YEARS! That made him a confirmed bachelor, right? That meant he was practically an antique.

Another problem with Kyle was he came from money. Garden party, private jet, and cars that cost as much as my parents' house kind of money. I know that doesn't sound like it should be a deal-breaker, but when you combine a much older guy with loads of cash, one word usually comes to mind. Gold-digger. (I'm calling it one word because it's hyphenated.) I can assure you I'm not the kind of girl Kanye West writes songs about, nor did I want to be mistaken for one. So for the past two years, I'd been telling Jayne no.

"Jayne, he's so old."

"I told you. He looks younger than he is. And he's a great guy."

"Then why isn't he already married?"

"Because he's waiting for you." Jayne winked.

"I'm serious. If he's so great, he should already be married. He's nearly forty years old, for crying out loud."

"Exaggerate much? He's only thirty-five."

"Same thing."

Jayne rolled her eyes. "You're impossible. If you won't go out for you, consider it an act of charity."

"That's not funny. I don't want to date as an act of charity."

Jayne leaned forward, her voice suddenly serious. "Okay, Charlotte. Here's the deal. Kyle has been Trent's friend since long before Trent and I got married, and I like him. I want him to find a nice wife, and if it can't be you because of your little hang-up with his age and the fact that he's rich, then I want it to be with someone else. Soon. So I need you to go out with him."

I didn't mean to, but I snorted. She was serious. She wanted me to go out with him so he could get married. Who cared what it did to me? Even though Jayne knew about my boyfriend-to-husband track record, there was no way I'd be telling her about the nickname I'd discovered over the weekend. Knowing Jayne, she'd probably have a nameplate made, and I'd have "The Husband Maker" hanging on my door.

"You're being superstitious. And you're using me." I tried not to sound hurt. Why shouldn't Jayne's primary loyalty be to a man she'd known longer than me?

Jayne shrugged.

"There's no guarantee it would work anyway, you know. I'm sure I've gone out with lots of guys who didn't get married right after we dated."

"You say that, but I bet you can't think of a single one," she said and I sighed.

"Just go out with him. What can it hurt? Who knows, maybe you'll like him. If I weren't already married, I'd set myself up with him. I'm not opposed to a life of financial ease, with great vacations and a housekeeper to clean my bathrooms. Say yes, or I'll have to set up one of those awkward 'chance' meetings, and then you'll hate me."

Inside I surrendered. I was a hopeless failure at finding love for myself. I might as well try to help someone else. Especially a desperate old guy. "Fine, Jayne. Go ahead and set it up. But promise you won't hate me when it doesn't work out and he's still a bachelor four or five girls from now."

Jayne clapped her hands and squealed like a teenager. "You won't be sorry. I promise you're going to like him."

"You have to admit nine years is a lot. He was in third grade when I was born. When I was starting kindergarten, he was starting high school. When he was finishing college, I was in junior high. Ick."

Jayne humphed. "Yeah, and when you're seventy, he'll be seventy-nine. Big deal."

I knew it sounded better the older we got, but I wasn't going to give her the satisfaction of agreeing with her. "I've got to get to work. These logos don't design themselves."

After Jane left my office, the horror of what I'd agreed to smacked me in the side of the head. I covered my face with my hands. I recalled a picture of Anna Nicole Smith smiling beside her ancient husband in his wheelchair and imagined me with my arm draped around an old man, dabbing at his drool with a handkerchief. I knew it was an exaggeration, but the reality didn't feel much better.

Chapter 3

*M*y apartment intercom buzzed. "Yes?" I answered.

"It's Kyle Aldsworth." He had a deep, rich voice in spite of the static that accompanied it.

"Great. I'll be right down." I ran to the window that overlooked the sidewalk in front of my apartment. I didn't have a great angle. The door to our building was narrow and sat behind a wrought iron gate between Cuddy's Clip Shop and Grandpa Guo's Shoe Repair. Cuddy's was two floors below us, and if guests were standing too close to the door, they were blocked from view by the barber pole attached to the side of the building.

Kyle stood a few feet from the door, allowing me a birds-eye view of dark, thick hair and a navy suit. If he looked up, I'd be able to see his face, which Jayne had compared to a clean-shaven Jake Gyllenhaal. Of course, if he looked up, he'd probably see I was spying out my window instead of coming to the door. I took one last look at my gray and white striped dress, grabbed my yellow cardigan, and headed down.

"You must be Charlotte," he said when I opened the door. I smiled and looked up—yes up—at one of the most incredible faces I'd ever gone on a date with. Jayne had been wrong. He wasn't a beardless Jake Gyllenhaal. He was Jake plus Cary Grant plus Captain VonTrapp, with a little of Jonny Lee Miller's Mr. Knightley thrown in for good measure. Perhaps that sounds ridiculous, but you weren't looking at him.

All intelligent thought abandoned me, leaving me unable to remember for sure what my name was.

What kind of game was Jayne playing with me? Kyle was much too beautiful for me. He'd have probably been too beautiful for Grace Kelly.

"You are Charlotte Emerson, right?"

How long had I been standing there gawping at him?

"Yes. I'm Charlotte."

"Whew! You had me worried for a second. I'm Kyle. It's good to meet you." He extended his hand and shook mine. His hand was perfect—good size, warm and dry, nice grip without too much enthusiasm. He was a hand-shaking artist. Great. He'd stopped shaking my hand and I hadn't relinquished my grip. I quickly withdrew mine and turned to lock the iron gate. My face burned, and I fidgeted with the key for a few extra seconds to give my cheeks a chance to return to their normally fair complexion.

Kyle was smiling when I turned back around. "My car's around the corner."

Grandpa Guo was sitting on a stool in front of the shoe shop, leaned over a laptop. He glanced up as we approached. "Ah, Charlotte, all dressed up for a night on the town?"

"Hi, Grandpa. We're going to a play tonight."

I liked our little apartment. I loved the tiny garage in the alley. I loved that it didn't have the fried food smell from a downstairs burger joint that Aleena's had. I loved our old-fashioned bathtub. But my favorite things about our

25

apartment were Grandpa Guo and Cuddy, the barber. They were both over seventy, but they were as different as chocolate and licorice, and I loved them both. Where Grandpa Guo was a short, stooped, Chinese man, Cuddy was a long, graceful Jimmy Stewart. Cuddy still cut a couple dozen heads of hair each day. Grandpa Guo had turned the business over to his two sons and now spent his days taking long walks around the neighborhood and chatting with people on the street.

"This is Kyle. Kyle, this is Grandpa Guo, my neighbor."

"Nice to meet you, Mr. Guo." Kyle shook Grandpa's hand.

"Yes, yes. So honored to meet you." Grandpa looked back at me and pointed at his laptop. "I'm googling best price for sports car."

"Are you buying a car?" Kyle asked.

Grandpa threw back his head and laughed. "No, no, no. I don't need a car. I live there." He pointed above the shoe shop. "And I'm here every day. I just like to look. But maybe someday I test drive. You enjoy your play. I'm going to watch this Bentley Continental on Youtube. It goes so fast I hope they don't wreck it."

"Have a good night, Grandpa."

"He's got good taste in cars, that's for sure," Kyle said as we walked away.

"I don't even know what a Bentley Constitution is," I said.

Kyle laughed. "Continental. It's a Bentley Continental."

I laughed too. "I'm not much of a car girl, I guess."

I stole as many glances in his direction as I dared on our walk to the car. Jayne was right. He carried his age well. There was no gray mixed in with his dark, wavy hair and his face was smooth and free of any noticeable wrinkles, except

26

when he laughed. The wrinkles that sprung up around his eyes when that happened were just plain fantastic.

The biggest clue he had me by nine years and at least seven figures was the way he was accessorized. His suit looked like it cost more than my car, and although I don't usually take note of watches, his was a sleek, brushed platinum.

And his car! It was the color of the lead in a graphite pencil and looked like something James Bond would drive. I imagined it throwing poisoned arrows or sprouting wings if we found ourselves confronted by an arms dealer or an international drug lord during the course of the evening.

"Is this what a Bentley Continental looks like?" I asked.

Kyle smiled. "No, this is what a Porche Panamera looks like." He opened my door and I slid into the plush, beige leather seats.

"I made us reservations at Urban Table," Kyle said after he turned on the ignition. "It's only a few blocks from the Curran, so I thought if you were wearing sensible shoes, we could walk." He glanced down at my yellow flats.

"Sensible shoes is my middle name." I cringed at my clumsy joke and reminded myself I wasn't very funny. Wait. He was laughing. "Anyway, I'm pretty tall, so I find it more sensible to wear sensible shoes. That way I'm not towering over everyone. Although I wouldn't be towering over you since you're pretty tall, too."

Close your mouth, Charlotte! What is wrong with you?

We pulled up to the curb in front of the restaurant, and Kyle got out, leaving the engine running. As he helped me out of the car, a valet hopped into the driver's side. The young man drove responsibly and carefully around the corner, before shifting to a lower gear, revving the engine, and peeling out. I looked at Kyle to see if he was angry. He shrugged. "They do that all the time."

"It doesn't upset you?" I asked.

"It's a fast car. They probably can't help it."

Kyle was so good to look at, I had to force my eyes to take in my surroundings. The dimly-lit restaurant was mostly gray and stainless steel with yellow and red modern art on the walls and tiny, frosted vases on each table that held a single, red poppy.

I watched him as he studied the menu. He was so smooth and polished and buffed that I wanted to be put off, but his smile was disarming, and he had enough of a Roman nose to avoid being pretty. Most of all though, he seemed genuinely nice.

My dinner of maple glazed duck with herb-roasted potatoes was scrumptious and probably cost about the same amount as the GNP of Kiribati.

"Can we offer you dessert?" The waiter handed me a gold-tassled card with the words "Dessert Offerings" at the top. One glance at the day's offerings had me crossing my fingers he wasn't one of those no-thank-you-to-dessert guys.

"Do you like hazelnut?" Kyle asked, and I gave a mental fist pump. "Because they have a hazelnut and chocolate soufflé that is out of this world."

"Mmm. That sounds delicious."

"We'll take two of them." Kyle said and handed the waiter his menu.

We compared our educational background and jobs as we waited for dessert. It sounds boring, but it was actually quite a stimulating conversation. Twenty minutes later, the waiter brought us two of the fluffiest, richest desserts I'd ever tasted. Each bite dissolved in my mouth, before bursting into a chocolate and nut carnival. I'd never cried over food before, but I felt precariously close to tears as I slowly finished mine, grateful he'd ordered two of them so I didn't have to share. With great effort, I resisted the urge to lick the dish.

"You were right. That was perfect," I said.

The three-block walk to the Curran Theater was easy in my sensible shoes, and Kyle graciously removed the awkwardness of the usual do-we-hold-hands-or-not-and-if-not-how-do-we-keep-our-hands-from-bumping-into-each-other-in-an-embarrassing-way dilemma by taking my hand and placing it in the crook of his arm. It was a gesture he probably learned at prep school or a manners workshop, but I appreciated it, and the walk was comfortable and pleasant. The slanting evening lights sparkled off windows and gave the street a golden glow.

The play was a little dull, but I didn't care. I was much too focused on the part of our upper arms that touched most of the evening. Was he purposely leaning a little toward me, or was that how he filled out his seat? I hoped he didn't catch me glancing at him and his ever-so-slightly imperfect, but exceptionally pleasing nose. His profile was an artist's dream.

His impeccable manners reappeared at my front door when Kyle took both my hands in his before I could even wonder how we'd end the date. "I think I owe Jayne a thank you. I had a great time."

I winced. "I probably owe her an apology." Kyle gave me a questioning look. "I might have dragged my feet a little about being set up. No offense."

Kyle laughed. "None taken. But I'm glad you agreed."

"So am I. Thanks for a lovely evening. And the best dessert I've had in months."

He squeezed my hands and gave me a quick kiss on the cheek. There was nothing romantic or passionate about the gesture, but it still managed to leave me short of breath and hoping I'd see Kyle Aldsworth again.

It was my birthday. Which meant it was Will's birthday. I'd worried this would be our first year celebrating separately, but fortunately, Will and Gina had returned from a job hunting trip on the east coast, and we'd be able to turn twenty-six in the same house. We were celebrating at Dad and Mom's house in Fairfield. McKayla and Connor were coming down from Mill City for the occasion, and Angus had promised to stop in with his new girlfriend as soon as they finished a round of golf.

Traffic was heavy, and what usually took about forty minutes was taking almost twice that. I didn't mind. I was listening to good music and thinking about Kyle. I'd been sitting in my office this morning when my phone chimed. The incoming text came from a number I didn't recognize.

415-555-2338: Is it true today is your birthday?

Me: Who is this?

415-555-2338: You mean to tell me you haven't saved my number in your phone yet? Ouch! This is Kyle.

Me: Sorry. Yes, it's true that today's a special day. It's the day my brother was born. ☺ How did you know?

Kyle: Jayne told me. You're a twin? I always wanted a twin brother. Lucky you. Are you doing anything fun to celebrate?

Me: This afternoon I'm driving to my parents' house in Fairfield so we can all celebrate together.

Kyle: That's great. Maybe we can celebrate again this weekend? If you're not busy.

Me: Hmm. I had big plans to clean out the fridge, but I could be persuaded to change those for the right offer.

Kyle: I'm feeling a lot of pressure, but I'll do my best to come up with something better than tossing out old food.

Me: I can't wait to hear what you come up with.

Kyle: I'll call you with the plans. Happy birthday. Eat a piece of cake for me.

Me: Maybe I'll save you one. Thanks, Kyle.

An hour later, a bouquet of flowers arrived. It was a lovely bouquet—purple and white daisies and button mums. The card simply read, "Happy birthday! Kyle." The whole thing was small and sweet and not even a little pretentious.

Since I now had Kyle's number saved in my phone, I sent him a message.

Me: Oh my goodness. Forget the fridge. I love the flowers. Thank you.

Kyle: Mission accomplished. Looking forward to this weekend.

I glanced over at the bouquet barricaded in the passenger seat and beamed.

About a mile before Dad and Mom's house, I pulled into a supermarket. I had a birthday present for Will—concert tickets to Mumford and Sons—but I needed a card to put them in. As I passed the baby aisle, I stopped short. Was that CJ? I wasn't sure because the man looking at diaper wipes had a beard, and CJ had been clean-shaven the whole time we dated. But the height and build were right. I darted around the corner when he tossed a package of wipes in the cart and made my way to the birthday cards.

If it was CJ, I certainly had no desire for a reunion.

CJ was my first fiancé. I should clarify. He never gave me a ring, but we were as good as engaged. He'd grown up in Vallejo, a few miles from Fairfield, so when we met the first week of my junior year at San Jose State, we had an easy connection. CJ was a senior and already had a job lined up in the office at a steel plant in Fairfield.

He was a class clown with a brain and great style, and we laughed all the time. We fell for each other quickly and split Thanksgiving between our two families. On the drive back to school after Thanksgiving, CJ asked if I had strong opinions about rings or if I'd be comfortable with him surprising me. I kissed his cheek. "I trust your taste and I love surprises." That was before I learned there are some surprises that aren't very loveable.

The night before CJ left for a Park City Christmas holiday with his family, we went to a special showing of *A Christmas Carol*. After the movie, he unlocked the car door but didn't open it. Instead, he leaned against it and looked at me.

"What?" I'd asked, feeling self-conscious.

Christmas lights flashed off and on around us, reflecting in the windows of the car. "I've been doing a lot of thinking," CJ had said, "and when I think about the future, I see you there."

"You do? What am I doing?"

He laughed. "You're painting pictures, and we're cooking dinner together, and we're playing with a couple of cute little kids."

"Mmm. Are we happy?"

"Yes, very happy." CJ stopped and turned toward me. He took hold of my scarf, so close to my neck I could feel the heat from his hands. "Charlotte, I want to marry you."

"Really?" I wrapped my arms around his waist.

"I really do. My grandma told me when I found the right girl, she'd give me her mother's engagement ring. Since I'll be seeing her this week, I want to talk to her in person." He pulled me close by the scarf and kissed me. "I didn't want to wait until after Christmas to tell you. I wanted you to know my plans."

"I like your plans." We kissed. A lot. Enough that someone thought they were funny and told us to get a room. I was mortified, but CJ grinned and said maybe we would.

"How am I going to get through Christmas break without you?" he asked when he took me home. "I'm going to miss you so much."

"I'll miss you, too. But we'll call each other every day."

"Or twice a day," he'd said.

The phone calls had started out long and romantic. We'd talked about big things—the future, what our families thought of our plans, where we'd live. And we talked about little things—what we'd had for breakfast, music, and the college football rankings. We said we missed each other, and we whispered, "I love you."

"I think Chuck's in love," Will said one night when I came from my bedroom after a long phone call from CJ. He and Angus were playing video games, and I tucked my legs under me on the couch to watch.

"Oh be quiet," I said. "I'll take on the winner."

Will lost and headed to the kitchen for some snacks while I beat Angus at two rounds of Mario Cart.

"All right, Chuckers." Angus flipped through the stack of games. "It's time for Cooking Mama."

"No way. I hate that game."

"Come on, chicken. You beat me twice. I should get to choose the next game."

"I vote for Cooking Mama, too," Will said, walking in with a bag of chips and a box of Whoppers. "Two against one. Sorry, Charlie. Winner plays me."

"I'll leave it to you guys since you're both dying to play a girlie game."

"If it's such a girlie game, then why aren't you better at it?" Will asked.

"Come on," Angus said. "I'll let you choose what we cook."

I rolled my eyes. "You're so generous."

Angus browsed through the menu. "Do you want to make custard?"

"Huh uh. I can't break the eggs right." He continued clicking down the list. "There." I pointed at the menu on the screen. "Let's try the shrimp au gratin."

"Are you sure? That's pretty ambitious." I glared at him. "Fine. Let's go." Soon we were shaking our hands in the air, cutting the tails off shrimp and slicing butter.

I waved my arm in a circle to melt the butter evenly in my frying pan. "Oh no, I'm already burning the butter. Look at you, you've already got the shrimp in the pan. Forget medical school. You should become a chef."

"It'd sure take less time. Hey Will, we should let Chuck's fiancé know she can't cook."

"He's not my fiancé, and I can cook. Just not on this stupid video game."

"I thought he told you he wants to marry you."

"He did."

"Sounds like a fiancé to me."

"He hasn't given me a ring yet." I wanted to put a stop

34

to their incessant teasing. The edges of my shrimp were starting to char and I knew Angus was trying to distract me. "It's not official until I have a ring."

"That's just a formality." Angus was now sprinkling herbs over his grilled shrimp. "Aaaaand, I win." He threw his arms up in the air.

"Maybe you should have Angus make your wedding cake." Will took the controller from my hand. "All right, Angus. Bring on the custard."

Two days after Christmas, I noticed a change in CJ's phone calls. He was quiet, and he didn't ask me any questions. "Are you feeling okay?" I asked him.

"Yeah, I'm fine."

"You're so quiet. Is something wrong?"

"No. I'm just tired."

"What are your plans today?" I asked.

"Oh, I don't know. Just hanging out, I guess."

Several silent seconds passed. "You'd tell me if there was something wrong, right?"

"Stop worrying. There's nothing wrong."

The next day CJ didn't call at all, and when I tried his cell phone, it went directly to voice mail. I sent him a text that went unanswered before I went to bed.

It got worse after that. We only talked two more times during the break, and both times were clumsy and uncomfortable, and I had to drag every word out of him. Something was wrong, but CJ wouldn't tell me what it was. I had a sick feeling inside. I needed Christmas break to be over.

CJ didn't come see me when we got back to school. Two days passed, and still he hadn't come over or answered his phone. I stopped by his apartment twice, but he wasn't home either time.

"I wonder what's going on," I said to Hannah, my roommate.

"I'm sure everything is fine. Don't get weird and paranoid."

I tried not to be weird or paranoid, but I didn't understand what was happening. We'd been planning our future together just a few short weeks ago, and now we weren't even speaking. I cried myself to sleep that night. The next morning, as I looked at my puffy eyes in the mirror, I decided I wouldn't go to bed again without some answers.

That night I walked the several blocks to CJ's apartment and knocked on the door. His roommate, Doug, answered. "Hi Charlotte." Doug glanced through the open door of the apartment, looking so uncomfortable I almost felt sorry for him.

"I need to see CJ." I worked hard to make my voice strong. There would be no crying tonight. At least not until later.

"I'm not sure if . . ." Doug's voice trailed off.

"I'll wait out here." I shoved my hands in my pockets. "You can tell him I'm not leaving until he comes out and talks to me."

Doug left the door open, and I sat down on a boulder in a flower bed a few feet away. It was a bitter night. Cold seeped from the rock through my jeans, and the wind bit at my cheeks. I pulled my jacket closer around me.

"You can't leave her out there. She's freezing." Doug's voice carried through the open door. Finally, CJ stepped outside and closed the door. His feet were bare—my first clue this would be a short conversation. We stared at each other for several seconds before either of us spoke.

"Hey, Charlotte. How ya doing?" The line sounded practiced, like he'd rehearsed it over and over as I waited on the freezing rock outside his door.

"Is that a real question?"

"Uh, yeah."

"I think you can probably figure out how I'm doing. You want to tell me what's going on?"

CJ folded his arms against the cold. He didn't speak right away, and when he did his voice was quiet. "I'm sorry. I didn't know she'd be there."

He might as well have slugged me in the stomach.

"Who?"

"Jenny."

"Who is Jenny?"

CJ sighed. "We met up with some old family friends in Park City. I haven't seen her for years, and . . ." He stopped talking.

"And what?" CJ looked at the ground by my feet. "And what?" I said again.

"And we're dating." He started hopping back and forth, and for a moment I thought it would serve him right if he got frostbite.

"Oh, wow. Were you ever going to tell me?"

"I'm sorry."

I turned and started walking home. The freezing air turned my hot tears cold on my cheeks.

"Charlotte, can we talk about it?" he asked before I turned the corner.

"We just did," I called back, but I didn't turn around.

CJ married Jenny during spring break.

I didn't want to think about CJ on my birthday, so I turned my attention to the reason for my stop.

There were only three birthday cards in the store for twins. One of them had fairies on the front and talked about "the Magic Kingdom of Twindom." Nope. The second had a lame joke about sharing amniotic fluid. The third said something about looking in the mirror and seeing yourself. Well, clearly Will and I aren't identical twins, so that card was inapplicable enough to be funny. It came with a pink envelope that I traded out for a green one, and I headed to the closest cash register.

Bearded CJ lookalike stepped in line right behind me.

"Charlotte, is that you?"

So bearded CJ was the CJ I'd dated. Of all the stupid luck.

"CJ? I almost didn't recognize you." That wasn't entirely true.

"You look great. Are you living here in Fairfield?"

"No. I'm still in San Francisco. I'm out here today to see the family." No need to solicit birthday wishes from an ex. A quick look at a bag of Huggies told me CJ was probably a father. He noticed my glance.

"Did you know Jenny and I had a baby?"

"I didn't. Congratulations. Boy or girl?"

"Boy. We named him Charger."

I love it when guys give me a reason to be grateful things didn't work out. "Is that a family name?"

"No. It's just a name I've always liked. I've always wanted to have a son named Charger and a daughter named Poppins."

And the reasons kept coming. "Well, congratulations. I'm happy for you." I turned toward the cashier, hoping it was my turn.

"Are you, Charlotte?" CJ's voice was low and serious.

"Excuse me?" I turned back.

"Are you really happy for me?"

"Of course I am."

"I handled things badly, and I always thought you must

hate me. You know, maybe you'd make a voodoo doll of me and poke it with pins or rip off its fingers and toes."

"Do voodoo dolls have fingers and toes?"

CJ didn't laugh.

"First of all, I don't know the first thing about making a voodoo doll, and secondly . . ." I was about to tease him and tell him if I knew how to make voodoo dolls, I'd have made one of Jenny, but the look on his face told me he wasn't going to respond well to sarcasm. "Well, there is no secondly. I really am happy for you."

"Can I help you?" the cashier finally asked, and I handed her the birthday card.

"Take care." I waved at CJ as I left.

"You're an angel," he called after me. Horrified, I glanced around and saw several people watching me.

Thanks, CJ.

Chapter 4

O f course I was the last one to arrive at Mom and
Dad's. Even Angus's car was already there.

"Finally. Where have you been?" McKayla came
skipping out to my car and gave me a rib-crushing McKayla
hug. "I haven't seen you in forever."

"I know. We're awful. We need to start meeting halfway
for dinner or something." I stepped back and ran my fingers
through her short hair. "You look great. Where did your hair
go?"

"I felt like trying something new."

"I like it. It's very Michelle Williams."

"It's so easy. You should go short, too. I'll cut it for you
if you want. I brought my stuff. We could do it today."

"I could use a trim, but I have to be able to pull it up in a
ponytail."

"Yeah, yeah. That's boring, but if there's time after
dinner, I'll take an inch or two off for you."

"Let's make time."

McKayla waited while I signed Will's card on the hood
of my car and slipped in the tickets. Finally, I reached in the
passenger door and pulled out my flowers.

"Ooh, pretty. Although I'm not sure Will's much of a flower guy."

I laughed. "These aren't for Will. These are mine. I thought we could all enjoy them."

"Who are they from?"

"A guy I went out with last week."

McKayla raised one eyebrow.

"Okay, his name is Kyle. Jayne set us up. There's not much to tell. We've only gone out once. So far." I grinned.

"I like the 'so far.' Are you interested?"

"I didn't think I would be, but yeah. I think I am. I'll keep you posted." We were at the door, so I lowered my voice. "But let's not make a big deal about it to the family. This isn't really news yet. If anyone asks, they're from a friend."

McKayla grabbed my arm to keep me from opening the door. "Speaking of news, what's Will's big news?"

"What are you talking about?"

"Come on. Will tells you everything. Don't pretend you don't know."

"I really don't know what you're talking about. How do you know he has news?"

"I heard Mom talking to Gina in the kitchen, and she said, 'we can't wait to hear your big news.'"

"Well then, we'd better go in and get the news."

It was great to have the whole family home. I hugged everyone except Angus's date, who I'd never met before. "Hey, Charles, this is Wyatt."

"Charles?" his date asked.

"Wyatt?" I asked back. We all laughed.

"Charles is just one of Charlotte's many nicknames," Angus told Wyatt. "There's also Chuck and Chuckers."

"Pretty, huh?" I glared at Angus.

41

"Wyatt is actually my name," said the striking red head with porcelain skin.

"It's nice to meet you."

"You too. Happy birthday, by the way. Hope you don't mind me crashing your party."

"Of course not. The more the merrier. Besides, it wouldn't be a real birthday for Will and me if Angus wasn't here to sing off-key."

"I do it on purpose. I really can carry a tune," Angus said to Wyatt.

"Then provide us with the evidence," Will said, sounding lawyerly.

"Someday. Maybe I'll surprise you all and sing at Chuck's wedding."

"That would be a surprise." Will looked at me in horror. "Gus singing, not Chuck getting married."

Dad put his arm around me. "Charlotte will get married when she's good and ready." I wasn't offended, but Dad always worried about my feelings, and I loved him for it.

"How was your round of golf?" I asked Angus and Wyatt.

"It was pretty good," Wyatt said.

"She's being modest. She beat me by four strokes."

"Losing your touch?" Will asked.

"No, man. She's just good. She played in high school, but after today, I'm thinking maybe she should join the pro circuit."

"You were just off your game." Wyatt patted Angus's arm.

"Actually, that was one of my better games."

Dinner consisted of all our favorites. Or at least they'd been our favorites when we were about nine years old. We ate Mom's not-from-a-box macaroni and cheese (my favorite) and Will's chili dogs. It was a tradition I'd have been okay doing away with, but everyone else thought it was fun. Luckily, I'd never outgrown Mom's sour cream chocolate cake with poured fudge icing.

The family sang "Happy Birthday" to us. I think Angus purposely tried to sound as bad as possible because he grinned at me and bowed. We blew out about thirteen candles each, and ate cake and ice cream while we opened presents. Will loved the concert tickets. And so did I.

"We must be twins," I said when I opened my envelope from Will and Gina and found two tickets to Mumford and Sons.

"Hopefully you won't have any trouble finding someone to go with you."

"I volunteer if you can't find anyone else." Angus raised his hand.

"Don't worry about Charlie. She'll find someone." McKayla winked at me. Mom, who never missed a thing, saw the wink and gave me a questioning look, which I promptly shrugged off, knowing she'd privately insist on more details before I left.

We finished opening presents, and Mom started gathering everyone's dessert dishes. Will cleared his throat. "Mom, can we wait a minute on those? Gina and I have some news."

"Of course." Mom stacked the dishes on the coffee table and sat back down beside Dad.

"I have some news, and Gina has some news. Who do you want to go first?"

We glanced around the room at each other, and Dad said, "Well, how about the lady goes first?"

Gina smirked at Will before she turned to the rest of us. "Well, you know we went back east last week. Will

43

interviewed at law firms in D.C. and New York. Well, he's been offered a job."

Mom moaned. "I was afraid you were going to say that. Not that we aren't happy for you, but the east coast is so far away."

"If you got the New York job, then I'm taking the New York Methodist residency for sure," Angus said.

"Do you want to tell where you got the job?" Gina asked Will.

"No, you go ahead." It looked like they were trying to hold in their delight.

"All right." Gina lost her battle with her smile and grinned. "He's going to be a prosecutor in Berkeley."

"As in California?" Dad asked.

"As in less than an hour from here," Will said, and the room erupted with cheers and congratulations. I was glad no one would be moving far away. I wasn't ready for that.

"Well, that didn't make my decision any easier." Angus hugged Will.

"Sorry, Man."

"No problem. This is great news for you guys."

"Speaking of news," McKayla said. "You said there's more."

The room quieted, and Will put his arm around Gina. "This is even better news than the job. You want to show them what you gave me for my birthday?" he asked Gina. She fiddled in her purse for a moment then pulled out a pair of pale yellow booties.

"What?"

"When?"

"That's great news," Dad said. Mom covered her mouth with her hands and tried not to cry.

"You guys need to get busy so our little guy has a cousin

close to his age," Will said to McKayla and Connor.

"We'll get right on that." Connor squeezed McKayla's shoulder.

"It's a boy?" Angus asked.

"We don't know yet." Gina elbowed Will. "It might be a girl, you know."

"I know. I don't know why I said 'he.' I don't care which it is."

I was thrilled for them. I really was. I was excited to be an aunt, and Will and Gina would be such great parents. But it did give me a little pinprick to the heart to know I was nowhere near being in a position to provide a cousin for their new baby. What if they were finished having their children before I even found the right man?

I hugged Will and Gina then picked up the dishes Mom had put on the coffee table and headed for the kitchen.

"Berkeley's good news, isn't it?" Angus had followed me into the kitchen with his and Wyatt's dishes.

"Berkeley's great. Especially since they're having a baby. I don't know if Mom could have handled her first grandchild living a continent away."

"Yeah. She looked relieved." Angus rinsed off the dishes, but I caught him glancing at me out of the corner of my eye.

"I'm fine." I put the rinsed dishes in the dishwasher.

"You sure?"

"Yes. Thank you. You're sweet."

"Don't call me sweet. I know what sweet means."

"This time I really meant sweet."

"I'll never trust you and that word, so don't ever use it on me."

I laughed. "Sorry. I promise I meant it in the best possible way."

"I don't care how you meant it. If you want to call me sweet, I'll be resurrecting your prom pictures."

"I don't believe for one second that you still have those."

"Why would I ever get rid of them? Sometimes, when I'm feeling overwhelmed with school or my life isn't going so well, I pull those out of their safe place and look at them for a while. They always make me feel better. So I'd be careful if I were you, 'cause if you start calling me sweet, those little beauties will suddenly appear on every social media site known to man." Angus shot me a wicked grin, and I cursed myself for the thousandth time for not tearing the pictures into tiny pieces before I threw them away.

I'm pretty sure this whole conversation requires a little explanation.

My first date ever was to a Christmas dance. Keaton, a senior from my biology class asked me out by bringing me a bowl of mini candy bars with a note that said, "It would be 'sweet' if you'd go to the Christmas dance with me." He'd never spoken a word to me before, so I was surprised he knew who I was. I didn't want to go, but Mom and Dad thought it would be a good way to meet some new people, and they even offered to buy me a new dress and a pair of silver shoes I'd been wanting, so I agreed.

Keaton was always cracking jokes in class, so by the time the dance arrived, I'd convinced myself I'd probably have fun. We went with two other couples, one had been dating two years and the other had been dating since school started. The other girls were nice enough, but soon I realized something was off. You see, every time I said something, Keaton or one of the other guys would say the word "sweet."

"How do you think you did on the biology test?" I'd asked.

"Okay. That was a sweet test."

46

"I'll have the fettuccine and vegetables."

"I've heard their fettuccine is sweet."

"Those are sweet shoes," his friend said, pointing at my silver shoes.

"Thanks." For a moment, I'd been proud of my silver shoes, but then Keaton and the guys all snickered, and the guy who'd complimented my shoes punched Keaton in the shoulder. Suddenly I felt self-conscious about my shoes.

When we went to the dance floor, Keaton yelled over the music, "Sweet music," and after the dance, as we drove to Shane Mullen's house, he said, "Charlotte, you've got some sweet dance moves." One of the guys snorted, and I suddenly knew he didn't just have a thing for the word "sweet." I was the butt of their *sweet* jokes. I didn't say another word the rest of the night, and when Keaton walked me to my front door, he said, "You're a sweet girl, Charlotte. But I don't think you're my type."

I didn't tell anyone about what they'd done until after Keaton graduated and left for Stanford. I was afraid Will and Angus would end up fighting Keaton and his friends, and that would have been uncomfortable. I'd have probably kept the whole thing to myself forever, but our senior year, Will started saying, "Sweet," when anything good would happen, and finally I lost it. "Don't ever use that word again! Ever!" Of course, I couldn't react like that without explaining why I hated the word. Ever since then, the word sweet had been an insult among the three of us.

Until today, when I'd actually meant it.

Oddly enough, Keaton had never married. Perhaps that's because his jerkiness overrides my curse or my curse didn't happen until after high school. I'm not sure.

About the prom pictures. High school brings back such good memories.

I only went on two dates in high school. It might have been because I was awkward and several inches taller than most of the boys. I was already five feet eleven inches by the time I turned sixteen, and I towered over most of the guys. I even had Will by a couple of inches, until he flew past me the summer before our senior year. When I stood beside most girls, I wanted to slouch down to minimize my loftiness, but every time I did, I ended up with a backache.

Mom signed me up for a summer workshop called "Grace and Refinement: Becoming a True Lady." Most of the workshop was silly—learning how to sit down properly, walking like a princess, and how to apply makeup to highlight your outer beauty. But one woman talked about being proud of who we are and our own unique traits. She told us our appearance was the product of thousands of years of genetics. Kate's red hair had probably been passed down from a long line of Scottish redheads, Kesha's full lips were a tribute to her African ancestors, and my height was something the Vikings would have found most pleasing. I have no idea if that's true, but after she said it, I was less embarrassed to stand straight and tower above most of the guys I knew. I just pictured Vikings smiling at me.

I longed for one of the tall boys on the basketball team to notice me, and when I got an anonymous phone call asking me if I'd been asked to prom and telling me someone was going to ask me, I hoped it was Todd. Todd Hancock was six feet five inches and gorgeous. He sat a few seats in front of me and to my right in Spanish. In spite of my best efforts to pay attention to the riveting teaching of Senora Vasquez, my eyes were drawn to Todd's handsomeness over and over again. Unfortunately, he caught me gazing at him a few too many times, and I'm pretty sure he thought I was a stalker.

Still, I hoped he'd be the one to ask me. And then I found out Todd had done what tall, attractive athletes have been doing for a million years. He asked out a five foot cheerleader. I know, because she squealed with delight as she told all the girls in P.E.

Someone should pass a law requiring tall boys to date tall girls.

I wouldn't have minded my height so much if I'd been more athletic, but when the sporty genes were turned loose in the womb, Will had grabbed them all and left me empty-handed. Of course, he says I snatched up all the artistic genes. Too bad we were both so greedy.

I was asked to prom by James, a boy who was four inches shorter than me. You'd think my most embarrassing high school experience would have been the "sweet" date, but you'd be wrong. My most embarrassing high school moment happened at prom with James.

There were five couples in our prom group. When the photographer lined us up to take our picture, he put the boys in the back and the girls in front. After he'd arranged us, he stepped back and held his hands in front of him, creating a makeshift frame around the group. He tilted his head and closed one eye. "Hmm. I can't see your date." He pointed an accusing finger at me.

Then he did something that may very well consign him to that awful place where he'll weep and wail and gnash his teeth throughout all eternity. He put me in the back row with the boys and my date in the front row with the girls. AND THEN HE SNAPPED THE PICTURE. I was so humiliated I considered running away with the circus. Doesn't the circus pay people who are freaks?

I'm ashamed to admit it took seeing my date's red-faced grimace in the picture, before I realized he was probably even more embarrassed than I was. After having the courage to ask a girl four inches taller than him to prom, the photographer had made him feel four feet smaller.

I'd been so embarrassed by that picture, I came home from school and tossed it in the garbage. Angus and Will were microwaving leftover pizza, and when I left the room, Angus retrieved the blackmailable envelope of pictures and has held onto it to this day.

"Are you ever going to give me those pictures back?" I asked as Wyatt stepped into the kitchen.

"Maybe on your wedding day." Angus dried his hands on a dish towel.

"It sounds like I need to be invited to your wedding," Wyatt said as she wrapped her arms around Angus's waist. "Interesting pictures and Angus singing."

"Be sure I have your address," I said to Wyatt.

"Hey," Angus said.

I tugged on his sleeve as I walked past him. "If you won't give me back the pictures, you deserve to be embarrassed in front of as many people as possible."

Chapter 5

I prefer to know what we'll be doing on a date, but Kyle said he wasn't sure, so dress casual but nice. What did that mean to someone like Kyle? I wasn't sure, but decided I'd be safe in slim, dark denim ankle pants and a striped, peter-pan collared blouse. I was relieved when I looked down at him from my window. He was in jeans and a blue and white checked shirt. My clothes would be fine.

"Sorry to leave you in the dark about our plans," Kyle said as we left my neighborhood. "I wasn't sure I could get us in, so I had a couple of different options."

"Get us in where?"

Kyle glanced at me. "Cheese school? Please tell me you like cheese."

"I love cheese."

"Good. Then I'm glad Plan A came through. I'll have to save Plan B for another time." I gave myself a mental high five that he was mentioning future dates.

When I'd thought of Kyle the last few days, I'd remembered him as handsome, but he looked even better than my mind had rendered him. Maybe it was the barely-there scruff from a weekend without shaving, or the casual clothes, or the shirt that made his eyes look like sapphires. Whatever it was, the sight of him had my heart acting like I'd just finished a marathon.

Kyle shifted gears and expertly drove through the Saturday morning traffic. What was it about guys and manual transmissions?

"So we're watching someone make cheese?" I asked.

"No. We're making cheese. Mozzarella. And then we're eating the mozzarella we make."

"That sounds fun. Have you ever done this before?"

"No. My brother told me about this. He and his wife have taken several classes here."

The sharp scent of cheese greeted us when we walked in the front door. Dark wood lined the walls, and a woman with a sleek, gray bob greeted us. "Are you here for the mozzarella class or to choose a cake?"

"We're here for the class," Kyle said.

"You make cakes?" I asked.

"They're cheese wheel cakes. Many couples opt for a cheese wheel cake instead of a traditional wedding cake. You can see some pictures in the hall on your way to the class, and you'll also see some actual cakes on your tour. Go down that hall to the last door on the right. Giannino is already in there with some of the other students."

The pictures of the cheese wheel cakes were beautiful. If I didn't love dessert so much, it would have been tempting to serve a cheese wheel cake when I get married. But alas, I must have chocolate, so although they were impressive, my future husband and I wouldn't be cutting into a wheel of brie.

"Welcome, welcome. Choose a table and put on your aprons." Giannino could have been Santa Claus if he had white hair and a beard, but since he was bald and beardless, I guess the resemblance ended with his ruddy complexion and giant belly.

We chose two stools at the second table while Giannino finished his conversation with two women at the front table. White canvas aprons hung over the back of our stools, and we put them on before we sat down.

"I was worried you might not like cheese." Kyle leaned toward me, his arm casually resting on the back of my stool.

"As long as it's not stinky or too sharp, I love it. Will, that's my twin brother, likes super sharp cheddar cheese, but I'm not a fan. I like it milder. And mozzarella is great. I didn't even know this place was here."

"Welcome." Giannino stood in front of our table with his arms spread wide. "I'm Giannino. And you are?"

"I'm Kyle."

"And I'm Charlotte."

"Thank you for joining us, Kyle and Charlotte. Are you novice cheese makers or experts?"

"Definitely novice," I said and Kyle nodded.

"You won't be after today." He smiled wide, showing a chipped front tooth. "We're waiting for a few more people, and then we'll get started. He moved on to talk to an older couple at a table to our right. The man looked like Einstein with bushy white eyebrows and a mop of white hair that appeared to include some tufts from in his ears.

"How was your birthday?" Kyle asked.

"It was wonderful. I found out my twin brother and his wife are having a baby. Best present of the day. I can't wait to be an aunt."

"This is their first?"

"First one in the whole family. She's due in December. A Christmas baby. Do you have any nieces or nephews?"

Kyle smiled as he thought. "One of each. They both

belong to the same brother. The rest of us are testing my mom's patience."

"How many of you are there?"

"I'm the second of four boys. Shawn's the oldest. He's married to Bethany, and they have Rachel and Jett. Then there's me. No wife or children yet. Then Pete. He's married to Danielle. They've been married six years. I don't know if she wants to have any kids. The youngest is Alex. Where do you fit into your family?"

"Will and I are twins, but I've got him by ten minutes, and McKayla is four years younger than us. They're both married—Will to Gina and McKayla to Connor.

"Where do they—"

"Good morning, cheese makers." Giannino's voice was as big as his grin. He stood with his hands clasped over his generous middle. "Today we're making mozzarella." He had no accent except on the word mozzarella, which was almost unrecognizable. According to Giannino, we were making "motezadayya."

"When I was a little boy in Oakland, I told my momma, 'I can't decide if I want to be a baseball player or a chef,' and she said, 'Son, I think you'll be taken more seriously if you become a chef. There aren't many baseball players with names like Giannino Annunziato. She was right, but to be fair, she could have said that about almost any profession, although it does sound better to say Giannino Annunziato, master motezadayya maker"—he kissed his right fingers and thumb and threw them in the air Italian style—"than it does to say 'here with your traffic report is Giannino Annunziato.'"

Everyone laughed except Mr. Einstein.

Giannino explained what our stations were equipped with—a large pan of water heating on a hotplate, a bowl of tepid water in front of us, and another large bowl of brine. After we pulled on plastic gloves, we went to his demonstration table, and he handed each of us a plate of curd.

"Slice your curd into cubes, and put it in your bath of tepid water." When all the curd was sliced, we ladled out part of the water and replaced it with warmer water. The curds began to melt and stick together, making long, strings of cheese. "We're cooking the curds, but we don't want to raise the temperature too quickly or we'll spoil the silky, luxurious texture, and you'll end up with tough cheese. Keep working the cheese with the paddle. Good. Good. Now ladle out about half the water and we'll replace it with the gradually warmer water."

"What am I doing wrong?" Kyle asked me. "My curds are still lumpy."

"Maybe your water isn't hot enough." I touched my finger to the water on his hotplate.

"It's not warm at all," he said, putting his finger farther into the water. "What should I do?"

I laughed. "I'd try turning on your hotplate." Kyle looked closer, and I pointed. "It's right here." I turned the dial to a hotter setting. "Here. Use some of mine until yours heats up." I poured a scoop of my warmer water into his and then transferred more water to mine.

I lifted the cheese and let it slide over the paddle back into the water, trying to match Giannino's method. Three times we replaced the cooling water with warmer water until finally, we poured it in boiling. I glanced over at Kyle's. He was a step or two behind everyone else, but it was looking softer and smoother. "That's looking better. You're a cheese whiz after all." I groaned at my own joke.

"Please tell me you did not just compare me to a can of

squirtable cheese."

I shrugged. "I did. I'm sorry."

Kyle shook his head, but he was smiling. "Good thing you're an artist and not a comedian."

"Good thing you do something with computers and not with cheese."

Soon we both had shiny, smooth cheese that melted over the sides of the paddle. Giannino moved from table to table, checking the consistency of the cheese. When he was satisfied, he returned to the front of the room. "Excellent. Now you'll start making it into balls. You can make it into larger balls like this." He put his hands into the still-hot water and pulled out the cheese, working it through his hands like bread dough and twisting off a tennis ball sized piece. "After you pinch it off, you'll place it over in your salt-water bath. Since it's still hot, your mozzarella will soak up some of the flavor from the brine. Keep working the cheese until you've transferred it all. Any size is fine, and if you want to get fancy, you can stretch it out and make mozzarella knots." He pulled out a golf-ball-sized piece of cheese and stretched it out several inches, then knotted it twice and put it in the salt water.

"I want to make those," I said and broke off a small piece.

"I think I'll stick with the basics," Kyle said.

I stretched out the warm cheese, but when I tied it, the knot weighed down the middle, until I was holding two long, skinny strands with a sad little knot in the center. "Wow, you're good at this." Kyle watched as I tried and failed at another knot.

I laughed. "At least I'm trying the fancy little knots instead of wimping out like some people I know."

"Stick with what you're good at is my motto." At that

moment, the ball of cheese he'd just squeezed off slipped out of his hand and plopped back into the bowl, sending warm, milky water splashing onto the front of his apron, the table, and even a little on his face.

I snorted and then gasped in horror and embarrassment. Kyle laughed as he toweled himself off.

"That didn't go too well."

"We're a disaster," I said after I failed at several more knots.

"Don't feel bad if you struggle with the knots." Giannino was watching me. "It takes lots of practice." After a couple more attempts, I gave up and formed the silky cheese into one large ball and several smaller ones.

"We'll leave your cheese to soak for a little while, and I'll take you on a tour."

We removed our gloves and threw them in the garbage by the door as we followed Giannino out into the hall. For the next twenty minutes, we learned the history of the school and interesting facts about cheese. I'll bet you didn't know the most expensive cheese in the world is made from donkey milk and costs over $2,000 per pound, did you?

As we looked at a wall of cheese cakes (not cheesecake), Kyle put his arm around me and squeezed my shoulder. Einstein's wife winked at us, and I liked that we looked like a couple.

I sighed. Not only did his hand on my shoulder feel nice, but the more time I spent with Kyle, the more humble pie Jayne was going to make me eat. Kyle's age didn't make me feel uncomfortable. I barely even thought about the fact that he was nine years older than me, and if his loads of money meant fun dates like making cheese together, I could learn to accept that.

When we returned to the classroom, we wrapped most

of our cheese up to take home with us. The rest we were eating. Kyle sliced tomatoes while I chopped fresh basil. We mixed that with some of our smallest mozzarella balls. Then we drizzled it all with olive oil and balsamic vinegar. We gathered with the other students at two long tables in the back of the room. Giannino brought baskets of warm, garlicky bread that we ate with our caprese salads.

It had been a perfect date, and I was sad for it to end.

"Snort again for me," Kyle said on the drive home.

"I don't snort on demand. You have to earn my snorts."

"That Einstein-looking guy wasn't amused by your snort."

"I think he was more offended by your cheese-making abilities than he was by my snort."

"I don't know how he didn't at least crack a smile."

"Some people don't appreciate a good snort," I said.

"I'm going to make it my mission to make you snort again. Any advice?"

"I never know what's going to bring on a snort, so you're on your own." I laughed. "Is the word 'snort' starting to sound weird to you, cause I swear it's starting to sound wrong."

Kyle pulled up to the curb and took the car out of gear. "It's a weird word." He turned to look at me. "I wish I could spend the evening trying to make you snort."

"I suppose you could call your parents and tell them you can't make it to—whatever it is you're going to . . ."

"A dinner with some political contributors."

"Right. I'm sure they'd understand you missing that so you can try to make some girl snort."

"Yeah. It's starting to sound weird." We laughed again. "Another time."

"Definitely."

Kyle kept smiling at me, and my stomach had no trouble turning into a whole bunch of little mozzarella knots. "I had fun," he said.

"Me too. Seriously, so much fun."

I thought he might be thinking about kissing me, and I had a little trouble breathing.

And then a blue shirt with the name Carlos written above the pocket appeared behind Kyle. He knocked on the window, and Kyle turned away from me and pushed the button to open the window. *Way to ruin the moment, Carlos.*

"Sir, it's a load and unload zone. You need to load or unload and move."

"Right. Sorry about that."

"No problem. Thank you."

Kyle closed the window and turned back to me, grinning. "I guess I need to unload you."

"I'm going. I'm going." I got out of the car and picked up my Cheese School bag of mozzarella. "Don't forget to refrigerate your cheese."

"I won't. Talk to you soon."

I stood on the sidewalk and watched as Kyle's car turned the corner.

"Sorry, ma'am." It was Carlos, who had pulled his white van into the spot Kyle had vacated.

"That's okay." I headed upstairs.

I smiled and leaned against the door after I entered my apartment.

"Charlie, how's it going?"

I jumped.

"Graham?" What was Graham doing sitting on the couch in my apartment? "Where's Mia?"

"I'm right here." Mia came out of her bedroom in running clothes. She perched on the edge of the coffee table and laced up her shoes. "We're going for a quick run. Want to come?"

"No thanks." I looked from Mia to Graham and back to Mia. What was going on?

"We made some chocolate chip cookies if you want some," she said.

"Thanks."

"Okay. We'll be back in a little while." Mia pulled Graham up and they walked to the door.

"Great to see you, Charlotte." Graham waved.

I watched the door close in stunned silence. Graham?

The last time I'd seen Graham was almost a year ago. At the time, he and Mia had been dating for ages. I was so sure they were going to get married, I'd made an entire Pinterest board of ideas for the best bridal shower ever.

And then it was over. Mia had gone to Phoenix for a week to see her family. She came back fired up and ready to give Graham an ultimatum. Move forward and start making concrete plans for the future, or end it. Mia was shocked when Graham chose the latter.

"He wasn't supposed to call it off. He was supposed to propose." She could barely speak through her hiccuping sobs.

"Better now than marrying you, and then taking off after you have two or three kids," I said.

Seriously, the dumbest thing in the world to say.

But I was trying to be a supportive friend, and I was as

surprised as she was.

"I shouldn't have pushed him. I should have been patient and waited for him to . . ."

"To what?" I'd asked. "Why hasn't he asked you? You've been dating forever. What's he waiting for?"

"Maybe he's afraid of commitment. Or maybe he thinks he can't afford it. There's not that much money in retail."

"Mia, I don't want to make you feel bad, but he's a district manager. He's over five stores. If he can't afford to get married now, he'll never be able to afford it."

"You hate him now, don't you?"

"You know I've always liked Graham, but if he's going to break your heart, then yeah. I kinda hate him."

"You're a good friend, Charlie." Mia started bawling again. "But I love him."

I hugged her and rubbed her back. "Don't cry. Give him a week. He'll probably come crawling back, begging you to marry him and give him two basketball teams."

"Do you think so?"

"How could he stay away? Look at you. You're smart and adorable." I held her at arm's length and looked at her closely. "Well, you're adorable when you're not bawling and your nose isn't running." Mia laughed and blew her nose. "You watch. I'm usually right about these things."

I don't know why I said that. I'm rarely right about anything when it comes to dating and guys. Look at my track record. But Mia wanted to believe me, so she did.

I was wrong. Graham didn't come back after a week. Or even a month. I guess the magic time frame was a year. And now they were out running, and Mia looked happy.

Oh Graham, please don't break her heart again.

Chapter 6

*M*ia and Graham returned about an hour later, sweaty and laughing. "We're ordering Wok and Woll," Mia stuck her head through my bedroom doorway. "Want anything?"

"No thanks. I'll just finish up the meatloaf if I get hungry."

"Okay. You can join us if you want."

"I know. I'll probably just work on this job for a while."

I glanced at the clock a few hours later when I heard him leave. It was after eleven, and I was starving, so I closed my laptop and headed to the kitchen for a bowl of cereal.

Mia heard me and came to the kitchen, rubbing moisturizer into her face. "You don't have to avoid us, you know." I couldn't tell if she was angry or not.

"I wasn't avoiding you. I lost track of time working."

"What were you working on?" Okay, she was angry enough that she didn't believe me.

"I'm working on a bid for a show in Branson, Missouri. Want to see it?"

Mia sighed. "No. I just don't want you to be mad at me 'cause I'm seeing Graham again."

"Are you seeing him again? More than today?"

"Yes. He's missed me, and he wants us to get back together."

"Like 'let's get married' together or like 'let's hang out' together?"

"He wants to date me, but he doesn't know when he'll be ready to actually get married."

"So it's back to how it was before?"

Mia stomped the floor. "Why do you have to say it like that? You make it sound like I'm backsliding or falling off the wagon or something."

"Hey, don't put words in my mouth. I'm trying to understand what's happening."

"We're dating. That's all you need to know." She swung around and a moment later the bathroom door closed. Hard. Why was she acting like I was the enemy because I didn't want her to be hurt again? I'd eaten a few bites of cereal when I heard her fling open the door.

"And just so you know," Mia continued, back in the kitchen doorway, "I haven't been really, truly happy since we broke up, so it'd be nice if you were at least a little happy for me." A few seconds later, it was her bedroom door closing with a bang.

This was so unfair. I'd never said I wasn't happy for her. I finished my cereal even though now it tasted like mud. I rinsed the dish out in the sink and got ready for bed.

The light was on under Mia's door, so I lightly knocked. "What?"

"Can I come in?"

"Sure."

I opened the door. Mia was sitting cross-legged on her bed, crying.

"Hey." I sat down beside her. "If Graham is going to do

right by you, then I love Graham, and I hope it works. The thing is, I love you way more, and I want you to be happy."

"I know." She crumbled into sobs. "I'm sorry I snapped at you."

"It's okay."

She blew her nose. "I'm scared. This is what I've been hoping for for the last year. I've imagined him coming back and begging me to take him back at least a thousand times. And then it happens almost exactly how I imagined it, and of course I want it to work. I love him. But I'm scared. He really hurt me when he left."

"I know."

"But how can I not try?"

"I guess you have to. But Mia, you've got to make him win you back. Make him work hard enough that he actually deserves you."

Mia nodded. "I'm not totally stupid, you know."

"I know that."

"I told him I won't turn down dates from other guys unless there's a ring on my finger."

"You said that?"

Mia giggled. "Yep. And he said he understood."

"Way to go." I put up my hand, and we high fived.

"Are you ready to tell me I'm always right?" Jayne sat down, a smug grin on her face.

"What were you right about?" I asked, pretending not to know.

"I'll wait for you to humble yourself. I just ate lunch, so I know I can sit here longer than you. Mmm. Is this dessert?" She reached for the giant box of Jelly Bellys on my desk.

Jasper, the Jelly Belly publicity man, had sent me the box as inspiration. I was creating the graphics for an interactive tour visitors could take of the factory.

"Those are for work."

"How many flavors are there?" she asked, lifting up the top tray and tasting a green bean from one of the lower compartments.

"Fifty."

"I didn't like that one. Let me try a cotton candy." She popped a pink bean in her mouth. "I like that one better. Seriously though, Charlotte. Tell me I'm right and get it over with."

"Okay, fine. Kyle's a nice guy." I turned my face back to my computer.

"That's it? Kyle's a nice guy?" She ate a blue and white speckled jelly bean.

"A really nice guy." When Jayne didn't respond, I turned to find her shaking her head and filling her hand with candy. "Okay. I was wrong." I put the lid on the box and moved it to the other side of the computer.

Jayne leaned forward in her seat. "He's cute, isn't he?"

"Gorgeous is more like it."

"I know, right? And he doesn't look old at all."

"He wears his antiquity well. And he's pretty handsome. And he's taller than me. And what's with his wavy hair? I just want to run my fingers through it."

"Then do it. I'm pretty sure he wouldn't complain." There was the smug look again.

"Has he talked to you about me?"

"No."

"Oh." I was more disappointed than I'd expected to be.

"Not me, exactly." Jayne got up, retrieved the Jelly Belly box, and put it back on my desk in front of her.

"Has he talked to Trent?"

"Maybe."

"Yes or no? How old are you, anyway? I feel like I'm talking to a sixth grader."

"Yes, he talked to Trent, and yes, he talked about you. You were all he talked about." I tried not to look too pleased. "I think he likes you, Charlotte."

"Good." I bit the side of my mouth as I turned back to a list of Jelly Belly flavors. "Which flavors should I have be the tour guides?"

"What are you talking about?"

"For the factory tour? I'm having two animated Jelly Bellys on the little film they show at the beginning, but I can't decide which flavors to make them. I was thinking Berry Blue and Bubble Gum because I like the alliteration of their names and they're good colors together. But are blue and pink too obvious? Maybe I should go with something more unexpected, like Strawberry Daiquiri and Margarita."

"I wouldn't do that. Some people might think you're introducing the kids to mixed drinks. What about Lemon and Lime?"

"Eh. Too 7-up-ish."

"What are your favorite flavors?" Jayne asked.

"Toasted Marshmallow and Buttered Popcorn."

"You're weird."

"I know."

"But back to Kyle. Do you like him too?" Jayne asked.

I smiled. "Yeah. He's a great guy, and he doesn't seem a lot older than me. We had fun."

"I told you."

"But I'm still not sure about the whole money thing. And the political stuff. He couldn't hang out Saturday night because he was going to some fund raiser. If I keep dating him, I'll have to know a lot more about politics. And what if I hate his dad's views on things?"

"Then you'll be diplomatic and keep your mouth shut. That's what they all do. Do you think every husband and wife in government agree with each other's political views?"

"Probably not, but we both know I'm not always good at keeping my mouth shut."

"You'll be fine. Besides, it's his Dad. You won't have to be involved that much." Jayne stopped at the door. "Just be sure if you go to one of those events"—she giggled—"that you don't snort."

She disappeared around the corner. "He told you about that?" I called after her.

She didn't answer. Instead she snorted.

"Hi, Janice. This is Charlotte."

"Charlotte. It's so good to hear from you. I keep telling Angus he needs to bring you down for a visit sometime. Will, too. I miss you kids."

Angus's parents had moved to San Mateo the same year we graduated from high school. Janice's mom—Angus's grandma—had been ailing. Since she refused to live with Angus's parents, it was either put her in a nursing home or move closer to help her. When a house on her cozy, tree-lined street went up for sale, Janice and Dave had snatched it up. Grandma Doris had died three years later, but Janice and Dave liked the area, so they'd stayed.

"I miss you, too."

"What can I do for you?"

"This is silly, but when we were kids, you had an old video about a jelly bean learning life lessons."

"I can't believe you remember that."

"How could I forget? *Jellybean Takes Care of His Belongings. Jellybean Doesn't Cheat. Jellybean Brushes His Teeth.*"

Janice laughed. "To think I actually spent good money on that."

"It was pretty funny, and it wasn't a waste of money. I still sing the tooth brush song in my head when I'm brushing my teeth."

"Oh dear. I scarred you." Janice said.

"You probably saved me a few cavities. Anyway, I'm creating a tour for Jelly Belly, and I was thinking about that movie today and thought it would be funny to watch it again."

"Oh, Charlotte, I'm afraid that thing is long gone. We got rid of so many things when we moved."

"I thought that might be the case, but it was worth a try."

"You could check Ebay," Janice said.

"Maybe I will. How are you and Dave doing?"

"We're great. I'm still teaching, and Dave's still straightening teeth. A tour for Jelly Belly. That sounds interesting."

"Yeah. It's fun doing a job for something so close to home."

"You'll be able to go take the tour when you go visit your parents."

"I can see people's reactions without them knowing," I said. "Actually, that sounds a little scary. Maybe I don't want to see their reactions."

"I'm sure they'll love it. Hey, I was wondering. Do you have a few hours free tomorrow night?"

"Are you coming to San Francisco?"

"No, Angus is coming down to pick up some paperwork. I told him we'd mail it to him, but he said he wanted to come since it's been a few weeks since we saw him. Why don't you come with him?"

"Is he coming down alone?" I didn't know how much his parents knew about Wyatt.

"Yes. I guess he's dating someone but she's probably not ready to meet the parents yet, although I'm not sure it's fair that your parents have already met her."

"She came with Angus to our birthday party."

"I know. Your mom called me that night to give me the scoop. She said she was a nice girl. Did you think so?"

"Yeah. She's great."

"Well, Angus is coming alone, so you should come with him. I'll make a pan of chicken enchiladas and you can have dinner with us."

"That sounds fun. Let me talk to Angus and see if we can work out the timing."

"I'll plan on you. Tell him to call me if it won't work out. Hopefully we'll see you tomorrow."

"Tell me about Wyatt," I said the next evening as we drove to San Mateo.

"She's gorgeous," Angus said, and I rolled my eyes. "That was a dumb guy thing to say, wasn't it?"

"Well, I'm sure she'd be glad you noticed, but I already know she's gorgeous. I meant how are things going? Do you like her?"

"I like her a lot. She's smart, funny, better at golf than any guy I know. Oh, and she's gorgeous." He grinned.

"You guys are so shallow."

"I'm joking. I mean, she is, but that's not why I like her. She's a lot of fun."

"What does she do?"

"She's a corporate event planner. You know, parties, fundraisers, conferences. That kind of thing."

"I'll bet our little birthday party was a bit of a letdown."

"Nah." A dreadful pop song came on the radio and Angus turned it down so we could barely hear it. "What's going on with you? McKayla said you'd have no problem finding someone to go to Mumford and Sons with you. Does that mean you're dating someone again?"

"I've been on a couple of dates with a guy. Kyle Aldsworth."

Angus looked surprised. "Any relation to Senator Aldsworth?"

"It's his son."

"Seriously? It's not the Aldsworth that was arrested, is it?"

"An Aldsworth got arrested?"

"Yeah, last summer. Drunk driving, I think."

"Wow. I hope it's not the same Aldsworth."

"Look it up." I pulled out my iPhone. I'd never googled a guy I was dating before, and I felt a little icky punching Kyle's name into the search engine. I hoped it wasn't Kyle.

"Nothing comes up under 'Kyle Aldsworth arrested.'" I scrolled down the page. "Oh, it looks like it was his brother. 'Alex Aldsworth was charged with DUI and disorderly conduct when he refused the officer's request that he perform sobriety tests. Mr. Aldsworth locked himself in his car until his legal counsel arrived. His lawyer drove him to the San Francisco County Police Department where it was determined his blood alcohol level was .15, almost twice the legal limit.'"

"Well, at least it's not your guy."

"Two dates doesn't come close to making him my guy."

"You know what I mean. Do you like him?"

"As much as you can like anyone after two dates, I suppose."

Angus gave me a sideways glance. "Just promise me if you break up, you won't go to his wedding."

"I can't make a promise like that." Angus shook his head. "It'd probably be a nice wedding. If I got an invitation, I'd want to see the cake and the dress and the food. I'd be too curious to see what kind of wedding a wealthy senator throws."

"Maybe it'll be your wedding, Chuck."

"Stop it. Don't jinx me any more than I already am."

"You're not jinxed. You've just dated guys too stupid to realize they should be snatching you up. Maybe this guy's smarter than the rest."

I sighed. It would be so nice if Angus were right.

Chapter 7

"Are you sure this is safe?" I asked.

"We take people up more than two hundred days a year." Kip, the short, wiry man, looked more like a carnie than the operator of an expensive hot-air balloon. "You're not afraid of heights, are you?"

"Maybe a little," I admitted, downplaying my fear.

"Tall girl like you shouldn't be scared of heights," Kip said. I pondered that a moment and concluded it made no sense at all.

"You'd better hang on tight to her," he said to Kyle and winked.

"I think I'll do that." Without missing a beat, Kyle put his arm around my waist and pulled me close.

"You don't need to worry, miss. The conditions tonight are just about perfect. Small breezes and no gusts. And good visibility."

The drive to Napa Valley had been easy. Light traffic. Nice weather. I was starting to think everything surrounding

Kyle was charmed. If Kyle wanted it, the heavens provided perfect weather, and the highway gods parted the typically heavy traffic.

I wasn't sure how I felt about a hot-air balloon ride. The balloons always looked beautiful floating through the air, and I was sure the view of the valley would be stunning, but Kyle said the balloons flew between two and four thousand feet above the ground. You'd die an unpleasant death falling from that height.

The balloon stretched out like a flat, nylon river across a grassy field. It had to be nearly a hundred feet from the basket to the top of the balloon. Red and yellow stripes popped against the grass. Kyle and I stood off to the side while another man positioned a giant fan facing the opening of the balloon. The basket was tipped onto its side. Although it looked like a picnic basket from the outside, I was happy to see it was lined with steel bars and a rubber floor.

Kip lifted the opening of the balloon and the fan roared to life. Nylon began to billow in the fan-made breeze as it filled with air, turning the red and yellow stripes into lilting chevrons. It was a beautiful balloon.

"Want to step inside the balloon?" Kip asked.

We stepped around the basket to the opening. The noisy fan blew harder than I'd realized, and our hair and clothes whipped wildly in the wind. Inside, the balloon was like an enormous nylon room with a domed ceiling. Sunshine glowed through the bright colors, saturating the air with yellow and red. I leaned down and touched the fabric. It felt heavier than I'd expected.

Kyle leaned close to my ear so I could hear him over the fan. "You excited?"

"I'm trying to be. I'm sure I'll love it once we're in the air. I think."

Kyle laughed. "These guys know what they're doing. Don't worry." He held my hand as we stepped carefully out of the balloon and over the cords and cables.

A few minutes later, Kip pulled on a couple of levers. With a loud hiss, a long flame shot into the center of the balloon. "How does it not catch on fire?" I asked Kyle.

"Why doesn't it burn?" Kyle shouted to Kip.

"The first twenty feet are made from the same fabric firefighters wear. The rest of it is nylon." His leathery face broke into a crooked smile. "Sweetheart, I've guided over a thousand flights and never had a mishap. You relax and enjoy the ride."

"I'll do my best."

A few more bursts of flame, and the balloon began its wobbly ascent into the air. As it gradually rose, it continued to ripple and quiver until it filled out to its full balloon shape. As it settled over us, it gently lifted the basket so it sat upright. Kip, never letting go of the rods that controlled the flames, swung himself into the basket. "All right, folks, climb in."

Cut out of the wicker sides were small footholds. I climbed the two steps and swung my leg over the side. Kyle followed right behind me. The rubbery surface inside curved over the lip.

When we were safely in the basket, Kip released several more bursts of flame, and the balloon slowly lifted off the ground. We drifted up and toward a stand of trees. Soon we were level with the branches. A squirrel scampered the length of a limb and disappeared into a clump of leaves. The trees melted into green clusters as the earth spread out below us. The balloon made a long shadow across a field to our east as the sun lazily traveled the last hour of its day's journey.

The ride was smooth as we glided above vineyards,

orchards, and large estates with barns as beautiful as the houses. Sapphire swimming pools sparkled beneath the setting sun.

"If you look far out to your right, you'll see the Pacific ocean." Kip pointed west. "You kids are lucky. It's not usually clear enough to see that far."

I'd never seen anything like it. It wasn't like looking through the little window of an airplane with the earth speeding by. This was slow and gentle and quiet. The peace was occasionally interrupted by the hiss of the flames, but even that began to sound beautiful with the soft, gentle sky surrounding us and the stunning earth below us. I rested my elbows on the edge of the basket, taking it all in.

"You can move around the basket if you want," Kip said. "It's as steady as can be. It won't rock or tip."

I'm sure he knew what he was talking about, but there was no way I'd risk moving around. I hated it when someone rocked the seat on a Ferris wheel, and that was anchored to the earth and not nearly so high. I stayed glued to the same spot. Kyle's arm had been wrapped around my waist, and I was glad he was standing so close. "Isn't this amazing?" He reached for my hand.

"It's magic."

The next thing I knew, Kyle's lips were brushing my temple. I rested my head against his, and we watched as the sun turned into a gold ball of fire and reflected its rays off the windows of every building for miles, scattering the valley below us with jewels.

The sun slipped behind the watery edge of the world, and the landscape temporarily lost its luster. Within minutes, lights began to come on in buildings, and everything took on a more subdued beauty.

"Don't be alarmed," Kip said, which completely alarmed

me. "When I pull these cords, the top of the balloon is going to open up a bit. It'll let out some of the hot air, and we'll start descending." There was a soft whoosh, and slowly, the ground moved closer. "If you look over there, you can see our truck waiting for us. We're aiming for that field right there."

Now that the sun was gone, the ground looked almost black. The truck was driving across the field where we'd soon land.

The balmy evening and Kyle standing so close made me forget my fear, and I enjoyed the feel of falling slowly through the air.

A breeze picked up a loose piece of my hair and blew it across my face. I looked at the dark trees, now silhouetted against the fading gold sky and noticed the branches were blowing. Now that the breath-taking vistas were disappearing, I was eager to land and get out of the basket.

The large field stretched out in front of us. We were only about ten feet off the ground. This was a height we could jump from and live, I thought with relief.

"That wasn't so—" Kyle's words were cut off as a strong gust of wind pushed us forward and toward the ground. The basket tilted slightly in the air, and the bottom edge hit the field and bounced back up, throwing us backward. I grasped the edge of the basket as it hit again and tipped on its front side. I flew forward, my face and shoulder smashing against the ground. My left hand still gripped the basket, dragging me with it as it skimmed over dirt and rocks.

"Let go!" Kip yelled.

Out of the corner of my eye, I saw Kyle tumble out of the basket and disappear behind us.

"You have to let go!"

In slow motion, I realized he was talking to me, and I

released my grip. My body crumpled over the side, and the basket scraped over my back and shoulders, driving my head into the dirt.

When my momentum stopped, I held perfectly still. Out of the corner of my eye, I saw the balloon move farther away, Kip and the other man hanging on to the cords and digging their heels into the field. They yelled and swore, but the words drifted away from me.

What had happened? I knew I was hurt, but I wasn't sure where. My back and shoulder stung. Had I landed in water? Why was my face so wet?

"Charlotte, Charlotte, are you okay?" I could hear Kyle somewhere behind me. Then he was kneeling beside me. "Oh no. Charlotte, are you okay? I need help!" he yelled. "She's bleeding."

So it wasn't water on my face. It was blood.

I dragged myself to my knees, wincing at the pain. "No, don't get up. They're bringing help. Hold still." Kyle sat on the ground and carefully rested my head on his lap.

"Here. Hold this against it," Kip handed Kyle some kind of cloth. Kyle pushed the rag against my forehead, and I cried out at the jolt of pain. I tried to push his hand away, but he held it firmly. Gradually it dulled, and I let him keep it there, my hand holding onto his wrist.

"I'm so sorry," Kyle said.

I don't know how long we sat in the dark field. I heard a siren and opened my eyes to see red lights flashing across Kyle's worried face. Soon, a man and woman put me on a stretcher and lifted me into the back of the brightly lit ambulance.

"I want to ride with her." Kyle was already climbing in the back with me.

"Sure, Mr. Aldsworth." How did the woman know his name?

I moaned as the ambulance bounced across the field. My mind seized on little details around me and little snatches of conversation.

Kyle had a scrape along the side of his face, and his normally perfect hair was caked with mud.

"She's going to need stitches."

"Could have a concussion."

"Dad, we were in an accident." Kyle was talking into his phone.

"Is he Senator Aldsworth's son?" asked a man, and the woman nodded.

The bouncing stopped as the ambulance pulled onto a paved road.

I licked my dry lips and realized I had a fat lip.

A sliver of light split the room as Mia opened the door.

"Hey," I said from my bed.

"You awake?"

"Yeah." My voice cracked, and my body ached, but I was glad for some company.

"How are you feeling?"

"Okay."

"What hurts?"

"I think everything." Mia turned on the lamp by my bed, and I closed my eyes for a moment against the sudden light.

"Is that too bright?"

"No. It's fine."

"Oh, Charlotte. If you wanted to be a celebrity, I could have suggested less painful ways to go about it." Mia smiled.

"What do you mean?"

"You're all over the news."

"You've got to be kidding." I pushed myself up, and Mia arranged a pillow behind my back. "Must be a slow news day."

"You're officially being called Kyle Aldsworth's girlfriend. One story even said fiancé."

I tried to laugh. "After three dates? That Kyle's quite a mover."

"Speaking of Kyle, he stayed as long as your parents last night, but when they left, your Dad suggested it would look better if he left, too." That sounded like Dad. Always looking out for my good reputation. "Your Mom is coming back sometime this morning. I'm still not sure why you didn't want to go home with them last night. You're so beat up. You should let her take care of you for a few days."

"I was hurting too much last night to think about moving anymore. I just wanted to sleep. I'll see how I'm doing today. Maybe I'll call Jayne and see if she's okay if I work from home for a few days."

"You sure you feel like working?"

"Right now I hardly feel like breathing." I put my hand up to my aching head. "What did they say on the news?"

"Hang on. I'll read you an article from the paper this morning."

Mia returned a minute later and started reading. "'Senator Aldsworth's Son and Girlfriend in Serious Balloon Accident.'"

"It already sounds ridiculous," I said.

"Oh, it gets better, believe me." Mia continued to read.

Kyle Aldsworth, second son of Senator Donald Aldsworth, and his girlfriend, Charlotte Emerson, were injured in a hot-air balloon accident west of Napa last evening, when a gust of wind smashed the basket and balloon into the ground. Mr. Aldsworth sustained minor injuries when he was thrown from the basket. He suffered abrasions to the face and arms. Ms. Emerson's injuries were more serious—a laceration to the forehead and lip, contusions on her arm and hand, and two bruised ribs.

Senator Aldsworth insisted a plastic surgeon be called in to treat Ms. Emerson's lacerations. 'We are deeply troubled that an activity that should have been safe caused the injury of a family friend and wanted to take every measure possible to see to it Charlotte's injuries receive the best possible care.'

Mr. Aldsworth and Ms. Emerson were treated at a local hospital and released.

Balloon Master Tours could not be reached for comment.

Mia folded up the paper. "Have you met Senator Aldsworth?"

"No, but it's nice to know he already considers me a family friend."

Mia shook her head. "Politicians. Kyle wanted me to call him when you were up to seeing people. Do you want me to call him now?"

"Not yet. I must look a mess."

"Yeah, you kinda do."

"Maybe Mom can help me get cleaned up, and then we can call Kyle later."

"No problem. Graham and I are planning to go out tonight. Do you want me to cancel?"

I gingerly shook my head. "No. I'll probably be in Fairfield by tonight anyway."

"If you're sure."

Kyle wanted to come see me, but I discouraged him until the next day, which meant he had to drive to Fairfield. He didn't mind.

"Come in, Kyle. She's in the family room." Mom showed him in then disappeared into the kitchen.

"Hey there." He was holding a bouquet of spring flowers. "Looks like someone's trying to outdo me." He nodded toward the giant bouquet on the coffee table.

"That's from your parents." Kyle laughed and put his bouquet beside the larger one.

I was stretched out on the couch, pillows under my head.

"Nice pajamas." He pointed at my pink flannel pajamas with Eiffel Towers and Arc de Triumphe landmarks all over them. "Been to Paris?"

"Nope. Mia got these for me when she went there with her mom last year."

"Maybe we can go someday and take a hot-air balloon ride over the city."

I groaned. "I'll pass, thanks."

"Can I sit down?" Kyle motioned toward the end of the couch. I tried not to grimace as I bent my legs to make a spot for him to sit. He gently pulled my legs onto his lap and shifted slightly to face me. "How are you feeling?"

"Better than yesterday," I said.

"Charlotte, I'm so sorry about this."

I shook my head. "It wasn't your fault. Accidents happen."

"I know, but I feel terrible."

"It wasn't you're fault. Don't worry about it. Until the final few seconds, it had been a perfect date."

Kyle reached his hand across my stomach and held my

hand. "Can I do anything for you?"

"No. I'll be fine. Mom's taking good care of me, and I'll be good enough to go back to work in a few days. Are you okay?" The side of Kyle's face was scabbed over.

"Oh sure. Mine is nothing compared to yours. That's what's so frustrating. I wish we could have traded injuries." His thumb brushed gently over my knuckles, and his other arm rested on my legs. He sighed and leaned his head back.

"Is something wrong?" I asked.

Kyle sighed again. "Charlotte, I have to ask you something, and I don't want to upset you."

I was confused. "Okay."

"My father wanted to come with me today. To see you. I told him I'd handle it on my own. You didn't need an Aldsworth entourage descending on you when you're miserable." Kyle looked uncomfortable.

"What did he want?" I asked.

Kyle hesitated a moment and then barreled ahead. "He's worried you're going to sue us." My surprise must have registered on my face. "I mean, you probably could since I'm the one who dragged you out there, and you got hurt. We definitely have more money than the hot-air balloon company, so if you were going to sue, Dad says we'd be the likely target, and he wanted me to tell you if you have anything you need, you should ask him rather than go to a lawyer."

I was stunned. I didn't speak for a long time as I tried to process this strange way of reacting to an accident. Of course, I knew people sued other people, but neither Kyle nor his father had been flying the balloon. Besides, it was a gust of air, not Kip or Kyle that had slammed the basket into the ground.

"I have no intention of suing anyone, Kyle. In a few

weeks, I'll be good as new. Didn't you hear the doctor?"

"Please don't be upset. He was just concerned."

"Tell him thanks for his concern, and you can put his mind at ease. I'm not chasing ambulances. Not even my own."

Kyle gave me a half smile. "You're a tough girl, Charlotte."

"You guys want me to put on a movie?" Mom asked from the doorway.

"You up for that?" Kyle asked.

"I don't know if I can stay awake, but we can give it a try."

Mom moved the bouquets to the fireplace hearth so I could see the television, and we picked a movie.

I fell asleep about halfway through *Spiderman*. When it was over, Kyle carefully lifted my legs off his lap.

"You leaving?" I asked.

"You need to rest. Can I come back tomorrow?"

"Want to come watch the Warriors' playoff game?"

"Sure." He leaned over and gently brushed the hair away from my bandaged forehead. "See you tomorrow," he said and softly kissed my lips. I touched my lips after he'd left, wanting to hold onto the feeling for as long as possible.

Chapter 8

"Since when are you dating the senator's son?" Aleena said when I answered the phone.

"Aren't you even going to say hello?" I asked.

"Hello, Charlotte."

"Hi, Aleena."

"Now tell me how long you've been dating Kyle Aldsworth."

I laughed, but stopped when my ribs hurt. "How are you?" I asked her.

"What? Can you not talk? Are you with the senator and his son right now?"

"You're crazy. No, I'm not with them. Of course I can talk, but try not to make me laugh. I'm in pain. What do you want to know?"

Aleena let out an exasperated sigh. "Everything, of course."

"We've been on three dates. Well, four or five if you count watching movies or basketball games together."

"Wow, I let a few weeks go by without checking in with you and you turn famous on me," Aleena said.

"I'm not famous."

"Oh yeah? You must not be watching the news or reading the gossip columns. Did you know you made it into the *Enquirer*?"

"Oh no. Please tell me you're kidding." The last thing I wanted was to be on some tabloid.

"Seriously, you did. Not your picture or your name. Just 'Kyle Aldsworth's girlfriend.'"

"Since when do you read the *Enquirer*?"

"I don't. Unless I think I know someone in a story. Now tell me how you came to be Kyle Aldsworth's girlfriend."

"He's friends with my boss's husband. It was a set up." I twisted the fringe on the edge of the blanket that covered my legs.

"And?"

"And he's a nice guy."

"And?"

I smiled at her enthusiasm. "And I like him."

Aleena Li and I had known each other for nearly two years. When her Dad's Chinese restaurant had needed some signage made, she'd come to Fife. Jayne assigned me the project, and Aleena and I had been friends ever since.

"Even though he tried to kill you?"

"Don't believe everything you read."

Aleena laughed. "Dad says we'll bring you dinner."

"I'm in Fairfield until tomorrow," I said.

"Are you trying to tell me your parents don't like Chinese?"

"I'm saying you don't have to drive all the way out here to bring me dinner."

"I do if I want to see my good friend in her time of need, right? I don't mind. How many will be there? I'll bring enough for everyone."

"Kyle's coming tonight. And of course, Mom and Dad

will be here. I don't know about anyone else."

"Ooh, so I can meet the man himself. I'll be there at six."

Mom stepped into the room, the house phone in her hand.

"They've tracked you down." She looked at the phone to be sure it was muted. "This is a reporter from ABC. She wants to know if she can talk to you. I told her no, but she still wants to know how you're doing and if you have a comment."

"No way." I didn't want to talk to a reporter. Mom nodded. "Do I say something?"

Mom shrugged. "I don't know. This is their second call. You were in the shower when they called the first time."

"Here. I might as well get this over with."

I took the phone from Mom and hit the mute button. "Hello. This is Charlotte."

"Charlotte Emerson?" a woman's voice said.

"Yes. That's me."

"This is Hadley Simson from ABC. Do you mind if we ask you a few questions?"

"I guess not." Mom sat down by me, and I held the phone between us so we could both hear.

"You're the Charlotte Emerson that had the balloon accident with Kyle Aldsworth?"

"Yes."

"Senator Aldsworth's son?"

I rolled my eyes. "Yes."

"Great. So, tell me about your injuries."

"My forehead was cut. My ribs were bruised. Some cuts and scrapes on my hand."

"And how has your recovery been?"

"Fine."

"Can you give me some details?"

"I've had some pretty good headaches, and I was sore for a few days, but I'm getting better all the time."

"Good to hear, good to hear. Can you tell us the circumstances of the accident?"

"Careful," Mom whispered.

"Uh, not really. It all happened so fast."

"Do you feel like the balloon operator handled the situation appropriately?"

I shifted in my seat and looked at Mom.

"I think so. Um, I think that's probably all I have to say."

"Ms. Emerson, one last question. Can you tell me the nature of your relationship with the senator's son?"

"Um, I guess I have no comment?" In all my life, I'd never been in a situation where I'd declined to comment. It felt so strange.

"Does that mean you're dating? Engaged?" The woman was pushy.

"It means I'm not going to talk to you about Kyle. Thank you for calling." I hit the end button and took a few deep breaths.

"That was strange," Mom said.

"Yeah. I didn't like it."

I texted Kyle and told him ABC had called. My phone rang within a minute.

"Did you talk to them?" he asked.

"Briefly. They asked about my injuries and my recovery. I told them I'm getting better. Then they asked about the balloon operator, and I didn't answer. Then I said no comment when they asked about us."

"That's probably best. If anyone calls again, why don't you refer them to my dad's office? They've been taking most of the calls."

"Have there been many calls?"

"A few. Nothing to worry about, though. Just refer them there. You don't need to deal with this."

"All right."

"How are you feeling?" His businesslike voice had softened.

"I'm pretty good today."

"I'm glad."

"I might try to go in to work tomorrow afternoon. I've got a lot to do, and it'd be nice to get in a couple of days this week."

"I'm glad you're getting better. Is it still okay if I come out tonight?"

"Of course. My friend, Aleena, is bringing Chinese food."

"I'll get out there as early as I can."

Aleena brought enough food to feed twenty. McKayla and Connor drove down to visit since Mom had told them I'd be headed back to my apartment in the city.

"I want to meet this guy," McKayla said before Kyle arrived.

"Me too," added Aleena. "Dinner was a small price to pay to get the inside scoop on Charlotte's fiancé."

"You guys knock it off."

"What?" Aleena should have been an actress. She had the innocent look down to an art. "I'm just repeating what I read online."

"We've only been on a few dates."

"I knew Connor was the one after only a few dates," McKayla said.

Aleena sighed. "You're so lucky. I've never felt like anyone is 'the one.' I've never even dated a guy good enough to want him to be 'the one.'"

This was crazy to me. Aleena was beautiful. She favored her Chinese genes with one huge exception. Her eyes were pale blue. She was so striking, she'd once been picked up by a modeling agent who had been ordering sushi behind her. She'd done a few photo shoots but had hated it. Even though her modeling career had been short-lived, one photograph had been used in a magazine ad campaign for yogurt. Aleena wasn't eating yogurt in the picture. She wasn't even holding a spoon. She was just looking pretty with strawberry yogurt floating in a thought bubble above her head.

Aleena was also smart and handled the publicity and marketing for the family restaurant. Most of all, though, she was funny. You couldn't help but laugh when you were around her.

"He'll probably be a fiancé soon. There's something about enduring a trial together that brings people closer," Aleena said. "I'll bet he acts more serious about you since the accident, doesn't he?"

"I don't know. Maybe. But how much of that would have happened with or without the accident?" I hoped his attention wasn't just because he felt guilty about what had happened. I was liking him too much for that.

"I guess we'll never know," McKayla said.

"There's an old Chinese proverb . . ." Aleena started, and I groaned. "What? I'm a quarter Chinese. I have every right to quote Chinese proverbs." McKayla and I laughed at Aleena's serious face.

"I want to hear it," McKayla said.

I shook my head. "Someday you're going to have to answer to your Chinese ancestors for mocking the whole Chinese proverb thing."

Aleena glared at me. "As I was saying, the old Chinese proverb says, 'they who travel the rocky road together arrive in paradise undivided.'"

"Ooh, I like it." McKayla nodded. "It's very profound."

"It sounds made up to me," I said. Aleena lifted her eyebrows and shrugged.

After Kyle arrived, I endured several awkward minutes of Aleena and McKayla's wagging eyebrows and annoying glances. Finally they settled down, and we had an enjoyable evening of food and games. It was the first time in five nights I hadn't had a throbbing headache, and I was able to laugh with only a little pain in my ribs. After a couple of games at the table, we moved to the family room, and Dad and Mom served ice cream while we talked. Kyle sat close, his arm around me, and I managed to mostly ignore Aleena and McKayla's several mischievous smiles that I'm pretty sure they wanted me to see.

"I think he might be the one," Aleena whispered as she hugged me goodbye at the end of the evening. "Does he have a single brother?"

"Yes, but I think he's a wild child," I whispered.

"So Dad wouldn't approve?"

"Probably not."

"Oh well. I'm happy for you."

I hugged her. "Thanks for dinner. Please thank your dad for me."

"I will. Let's get together for lunch soon."

McKayla and Connor left shortly after Aleena. "He's a good one," McKayla said. "Don't go scaring this one off." I glanced around, making sure Kyle wasn't in earshot. I knew McKayla loved me, so I tried not to be bothered.

"I don't scare them off, Mick." Why did so many people assume my failed love life was all my fault?

"I know you don't. It's just a saying. A really dumb one, come to think of it." She kissed my cheek. "I love you. Feel better."

After Connor and McKayla left, Dad and Mom headed to bed. Kyle and I snuggled on the couch and watched couples hunt for houses in New Zealand and Belize. When the last couple picked a terrible apartment overlooking an empty, weedy lot, Kyle got up to leave. We walked to the door, holding hands.

"How about something boring like dinner and a movie this weekend? You up for that?" he asked, holding both my hands.

"Boring has never sounded so good." Kyle laughed. "Good. Let's plan on Saturday. I'll give you a call. Take it easy at work the next couple of days. Don't push yourself too hard."

"I won't. I'll be fine."

"Call me if you need anything."

Kyle pulled me in his arms and held me close. His arms felt strong and gentle and he smelled like warm oranges. I wanted to stay there for hours breathing in the scent of him. He kissed my forehead before he turned to go.

I'm pretty sure the dizziness I felt when he left wasn't from my head injury.

Chapter 9

$\mathcal{W}$ hether it was following the course of an old Chinese proverb or it was just moving along its normal course, things with Kyle were going well. He'd put the big, flashy dates on the back burner since the balloon accident, and most of our dating was more conventional. We went to a couple of movies, a few nice dinners, and a Warriors playoff game, where we practically sat on the floor and cheered them on to victory.

My wounds had healed nicely over the past several weeks, and the only visible sign it had happened was a pink scar on my forehead the doctor assured me would fade with time.

"Do you like boating?" Kyle asked at lunch one day. I must have looked as unenthusiastic as I felt because he laughed. "Are we going to avoid every outdoor activity for the rest of our lives?"

Don't think I didn't notice his reference to the rest of our lives. I did, and I liked it. In fact, once I answered his question, I'd bask in the beauty of that comment for days. "Tell me more."

"We have a place at Lake Tahoe. The family's headed

over there next weekend for some boating and wakeboarding, and I want you to come."

Lake Tahoe sounded beautiful. Meeting the family and wakeboarding sounded terrifying. "I don't know. I've never done that before."

"That's okay. I'll teach you. I taught my younger brothers how to wakeboard and I taught my brother's girlfriend. I'll teach you."

I sighed. "What if I'm a huge disappointment? I'm not very athletic, you know."

"I've never failed yet. And you know I like a good challenge."

"Is it your whole family?"

"Shawn's family can't come, and Pete's wife is working, so it'll be my parents, Pete, us and Alex."

I was trying not to sound too insecure, but suddenly, working sounded like a perfect way to spend a weekend. I'd be meeting his parents for the first time and I'd probably make a spectacle of myself.

Kyle was smiling at me, and I couldn't help but smile back. He made it hard to say no.

"I guess I could try it if you think you're up to the task of teaching me." Kyle leaned across the table and kissed me. I was glad I'd agreed.

"I was hoping you'd say yes. I want Dad and Mom to meet you, and Lake Tahoe is beautiful. We'll drive up with my parents on Friday evening. We'll stay at the cabin, and then Saturday we'll spend the day boating. Dad has to be back for a Sunday morning news show, so we'll come home Saturday night."

"Sounds great." It didn't sound great. It sounded scary. When I say I'm not athletic, I mean it. When I tried skateboarding, I broke my arm. When we did a modern dance unit in P.E., I did a face plant in front of the entire class. Even something as simple as running had managed to humiliate me. We were on a field trip to the capitol building. The plan was to eat our lunches under a stand of trees. Mrs. Vindel pointed to the trees and said, "Last one there is a rotten egg." The class took off running. No one wanted to be last. I tripped on something—probably my own feet—and hit my head on a curb. Not only was I the rotten egg, I also had a giant goose egg on my forehead.

And now I was going wakeboarding with Kyle and his family. I took a deep breath. I had one week to psych myself up.

I'd only been home from work for ten minutes when Kyle rang the bell. Good thing I'd packed the night before. A black Lincoln Navigator was parked at the curb when I walked out. Kyle was talking to Cuddy and Grandpa Guo when I came through the gate, carrying my suitcase.

"Here, I'll get that for you." Kyle picked up my bag.

"This young man tells me you're headed for Lake Tahoe," Cuddy said.

"With his family." I pointed to the car where Kyle's family was waiting.

Cuddy chuckled. "Good, good. Glad you're going to be chaperoned."

"I think this one has honorable intentions," Grandpa Guo said to Cuddy.

"I definitely do," Kyle assured them.

"I hope so, son. Charlotte's one of our favorites," Cuddy said.

"She's one of my favorites, too," Kyle shook Cuddy's

hand and then Grandpa Guo's before carrying my suitcase to the back of the Navigator.

"And you're two of my favorites." I kissed their cheeks. "I'll be back tomorrow night."

"Have a fun weekend," Grandpa Guo said.

"But not too fun," Cuddy added, and they laughed.

Kyle helped me into the backseat of the Navigator. I smiled at my sweet neighbors, Cuddy standing more than a foot taller than Grandpa Guo. They waved goodbye.

"Dad and Mom, this is Charlotte. Charlotte, these are my parents, Donald and Roberta."

"Nice to meet you both." I leaned forward and shook their hands. I quickly did the math in my head. They had to be in their mid to late fifties, but they could easily have passed for somewhere in their forties. They were an attractive couple, much more relaxed than when I'd seen them on television.

"Wonderful to meet you, too," Donald said.

"You look great," Roberta said. "I was so glad you were feeling well enough to go with us this weekend. That was quite an ordeal you had."

"I'm doing fine. Thank you."

"And these are two of my brothers, Pete and Alex," Kyle pointed to the back seat.

"Hi, Charlotte." Pete leaned forward and shook my hand.

"Hey." Alex tipped his ball cap at me but stayed lounging in the corner of the back seat.

Traffic leaving the city was heavy, and progress was slow, but the conversation around me stayed lively. I was glad they didn't feel the need to pepper me with questions. I preferred listening. Occasionally they'd ask me a question, but mostly they talked about their jobs, their family, and politics.

We were west of Sacramento when Roberta put up her hand for everyone's attention. "Now, don't forget. I said you could discuss this session of congress until we get to the cabin, and then all politics stops, and we enjoy ourselves. So get this out of your system." She turned to me. "Sometimes we have to lay down the law, or all we'd do is talk about politics."

I smiled. It sounded like a good rule.

"We have about twenty-four hours to play and relax, and we're going to make the most of it."

Everyone was gracious and energetic. Well, everyone except Alex. He slept most of the way there. Kyle reached across our captain's seats and stroked my neck under my hair. If I were a cat, I'd have arched my back and purred, it felt so nice.

"We eating any time soon?" Alex leaned up between our seats, his face uncomfortably close to mine. "I'm starving."

"Margaret will have dinner ready for us when we get there," Roberta said.

"Sweet." He leaned back in his seat.

"Margaret and her husband get the cabin ready for us when we're coming, and she cooks while we're there," explained Kyle.

I nodded, as if I'd seen arrangements like this all my life.

The Aldsworths' cabin sat somewhere behind a gated entrance. Mr. Aldsworth pulled up to a keypad and entered a code. A robotic woman's voice welcomed us home, and the wrought iron gate swung open. Mr. Aldsworth pulled through and drove slowly down a paved lane. A small stream bubbled beside the drive as we climbed the side of a hill and rounded a bend.

In front of us was a rustic glass and wood home that looked out over a valley of wildflowers and grass. Behind the house was a forest of pine trees. Mr. Aldsworth pulled around to the back where the driveway opened up into a wide, paved courtyard. At the back end of the courtyard was a smaller house and a garage.

The cabin wasn't at all what I'd expected. My Uncle Paul has a cabin in Idaho. I went there once as a teenager. It was a log structure with one small bedroom and a loft where we could throw down sleeping bags. We'd been thrilled because it had a small, indoor bathroom with a shower.

"We're here," Mr. Aldsworth said.

"No more shop talk." Roberta undid her seatbelt.

We entered the house through the back door that led through a mud room and into an enormous kitchen with butcher block countertops and wooden beams high overhead.

"Welcome home." An older woman with short, salt and pepper hair greeted us.

"Margaret, something smells wonderful," Mr. Aldsworth said.

"I love you." Alex planted a kiss on Margaret's cheek.

"Of course you do. Especially when you're hungry." Margaret shooed him away.

"You're wrong, Margaret. I love you all the time."

Margaret shook her head. "Dinner will be on the table in twenty minutes."

"Kyle, take Charlotte to the yellow room and let her get settled in," Roberta said.

"Barry will get your bags and bring them up." Margaret sliced tomatoes as she spoke.

"Who's Barry?" I asked Kyle as we left the kitchen.

"He's Margaret's husband. They're pretty much retired. Did you see the house by the garage?"

I nodded.

"They live there and take care of the place. When we come stay, they take care of us."

We walked through a great room with what had to be thirty foot ceilings and heavy, leather furniture and then up a flight of stairs. "The guys stay in these." He pointed at a couple of rooms as we passed. "I'll be in here." Kyle opened a door to a bedroom with a tall, log bed covered with a red, white and blue quilt. "And your room is right here."

The yellow room was like something out of a magazine. A white four-poster bed sat in the middle of the room. A yellow, rose-covered quilt covered the bed, and an overstuffed, yellow chair sat in the corner. "This is so pretty." I ran my hand over the quilt.

"You have your own bathroom." Kyle pointed to a door that led off the room. "Does this look okay?"

"It looks great."

"This your bag?" asked an older man at the door.

"Yes, thank you."

"Thanks, Barry."

"No problem." He left the bag and pulled the door almost closed.

I laughed.

"What?" Kyle asked.

"This isn't like any cabin I've ever seen before."

Kyle smiled and put his arms around me. "I'm glad you came."

"I think I am too," I said, and he raised his eyebrows. "I'm still kinda dreading the wakeboarding."

"You'll do fine." He kissed me. "I've wanted to do that ever since we picked you up."

"You can do it again if you want," I said.

"I do."

I wrapped my arms around his neck and kissed him back.

"Want to join us?" Alex said, standing in the doorway. His voice sounded bored. "We're all hungry. For food." I stepped away from Kyle, my face hot with embarrassment.

Kyle laughed. "Let's go."

Kyle knocked on my door when it was time to go down for breakfast. The previous night had been fun. After a delicious dinner, we'd watched an old John Wayne movie and then played a few games. In spite of Alex's good-humored trash talking, I'd beat everyone at Yahtzee. I wasn't so lucky at Ticket to Ride.

I liked Kyle's family. Everyone, including Alex, had been pleasant and funny.

Margaret served pancakes and eggs for breakfast, and Mr. Aldsworth, who told me to call him Donald, announced we'd be leaving for the lake in an hour. I returned to my room and put on my swimsuit, shorts and a t-shirt.

Roberta knocked. "Do you need anything before we go?" she asked when I opened the door.

"I don't think so." I wiped my damp hands on my shorts. The reality that we were going wakeboarding soon was hitting me hard.

"Kyle says you've never done anything like this before."

"That's true."

"Don't worry. You'll do fine."

"That's what Kyle keeps telling me. We'll see. I'm not as optimistic as you two."

"If I can learn how, I'm sure you can too. And we're all friends, so you don't need to worry about us."

"Thank you." I appreciated her encouragement, but it didn't stop my palms from sweating.

"Shall we head down?"

The Navigator was sitting in the courtyard. On a trailer behind it was a sleek, red and white boat. It looked fast. I wondered if anyone would be suspicious if I said I was sick.

The trip to the lake was much too short, and much sooner than I wanted, we were out on the lake. I insisted everyone take a turn before Kyle tried to teach me. That was both a good thing and a bad thing. Good, because it bought me another hour. Bad, because I soon realized I was boating with what might as well have been the U.S. National wakeboard team. They were all good. Even Donald and Roberta. Kyle and his brothers jumped across the wake, and even though he crashed on his first attempt, Alex did a flip. As each of them took their turn, Kyle pointed out their form and gave me tips.

"If you start to fall, be sure to let go of the towrope. Then we'll circle around and pick you up."

"Be sure to bend your knees and lean back."

"Let the boat pull you up."

"Once you start to stand, dig in your back foot and swing the board sideways, the way you'd ride a skateboard."

"We'll pull the boat away from you slowly until the rope is tight, but we won't take off until you give us the signal."

By the time they'd all had a run, I was starting to think that maybe I could do it. How hard could it be if his fifty-something-year-old parents could do it?

Kyle helped me with the equipment.

With one more pep talk, I entered the water. I tried to keep my view of the boat over the board, but keeping myself steady in the water proved difficult. Peter edged the boat away from me until the towrope was tight then it idled as they waited for my signal. "Let us know when you're ready,"

Kyle called to me. I did my best to relax in the water, which was what Kyle had told me to do. I tried to keep my knees bent, but the buoyancy of the board made it difficult. Quickly, I lifted my hand from the towrope and gave a thumbs up, grabbing the handle again as the pitch of the engine rose. With all my strength, I kept my legs in front of me. I tried to pull myself up, but the edge of the board submerged, and I flew forward, awkwardly diving back into the water as the towrope was yanked from my hands. My first effort had made me feel like I'd just visited the chiropractic. I desperately tried to pull the board back around and get my feet in position before the boat came around to pick me up. It wasn't easy with both my feet stuck in the board. Kyle leaned over the boat and gave me a few pointers then Peter pulled the boat slowly away and I tried again. With the same result. I tried three more times before Kyle let me off the hook. "Do you want to try again right now or take a break?"

"I'll take a little break and let some of you board again."

I caught my breath in the boat, while Donald took another run. Roberta sat down beside me and patted my leg. "Don't worry, Charlotte, you'll get it with a little practice. Just keep watching and try to follow Kyle's instructions."

"Let's get her back in there," Alex said when everyone had taken a turn.

Donald drove the boat this time. "Now remember," Kyle said before they moved the boat away from me. "If you try to stand up too soon, the board will sink, so let the boat pull you up and keep your weight on that back foot. You can do it." I appreciated his enthusiastic tone and wanted to succeed for him, but after being dragged through the water three more times without successfully standing, Donald stopped the boat and slowly circled back.

I felt like I'd been on the water for days. My muscles were screaming at me and the fake smile was getting harder and harder to plaster on my face.

"You're so close," Kyle said. "Let's give it one more try. You're going to love it once you get up. You can do it."

I wanted to do it. I did. I didn't like failing, especially in front of people.

I was exhausted, embarrassed and determined that this time I'd get upright on the board. I tried to ignore the bleak glances Kyle's parents and brothers exchanged and gave myself a silent pep talk. I felt like I was single-handedly ruining their trip.

I shook out my hands one at a time while the boat crept forward and the rope became taut. Then for the last time that day, I held up my thumb. Donald gunned the engine, and the boat lurched forward.. It took every ounce of strength left in my rubbery muscles to keep my legs in front of me. I glanced at the boat, and Kyle gave me an encouraging thumbs-up. My legs wobbled, but I gritted my teeth and forced them to stay steady. Slowly, I lifted myself out of the water. I was upright. I risked a quick glance at the boat. Everyone was cheering, and Kyle was fist-pumping the air. Even Alex was smiling.

For about ten glorious seconds, I was a wakeboarder. And then the edge of my board dipped forward, and before I knew what was happening, I faceplanted into the hardest water I'd ever felt. Once again, the towrope was torn from my grip at the same time the board was torn from my feet, but I didn't care. My head pounded with the worst migraine I'd ever felt, and my entire body stung, as though someone had slapped me all over. I rolled onto my back and floated there, willing my head to stop pounding. When the boat came back around, Kyle looked worried, but Peter and Alex had turned away from me. Alex's back was shaking with laughter.

"Are you okay?" Kyle asked.

"I think so."

"You got up. Great job." He reached down to pull me into the boat. My arms felt like jelly, and I couldn't see straight. Halfway up the side of the boat, my wet hand slipped out of Kyle's, and I splashed back into the water. New laughter erupted inside the boat. My muscles quivered as we tried again. "Hey guys, can one of you come help me?" Kyle asked. Alex kept his back to me, but Peter leaned over the side with Kyle. Each of them took an arm, and with a grunting effort that made me feel like a dead hippopotamus, they finally pulled me into the boat.

Once I was seated, I felt the tears prickling the edge of my eyes. If I cried, I might as well throw myself over the side of the boat and drown. I'd embarrassed myself and Kyle enough. So I fixed a smile on my face and stayed that way throughout the afternoon as everyone else took a few more turns on the water. Kyle took over driving the boat, so I moved my sore body to the front with him. Thankfully, no one tried to offer words of consolation or comfort. Any extra kindness would have turned on the faucet of my tears.

Margaret had barbecued beef sandwiches ready when we arrived at the house. We ate and loaded up for the trip home.

Peter drove, and Kyle and I sat in the back seat on the drive back to San Francisco. We'd hardly spoken since the boating. Had I embarrassed him? Maybe he wanted to break things off and find an athlete. Maybe an Olympic beach volleyballer or a swimmer. Were Shawn and Peter's wives professional wakeboarders like the rest of the family? They were probably good at everything.

The sun was setting when we merged into the I-80 traffic. Alex manned the radio and Donald worked on his laptop, while Roberta fell asleep. I glanced at Kyle. He was smiling. I returned his with a small, sheepish one of my own. He unbuckled his seatbelt and moved to the middle seat. "Come here." He put his arm around me and pulled me into his side. I snuggled in and rested my head on his shoulder while his fingers moved up and down my arm. "You okay?" he whispered, and I nodded even as a tear slid down my cheek. I quickly brushed it away.

He pulled my arm around his waist and held me there in his arms. I realized I was holding my breath and tried to breathe normally so he wouldn't know how his touch affected me. Breathe in. Breathe out. Breathe in. Breathe out. Kyle felt so warm I wanted to burrow into him. His arm stopped moving. I held perfectly still, afraid any movement might change the mood and make him pull away.

And then his hand lifted my face slowly toward his, and his lips brushed back and forth over mine a few times before they settled there. It was an unhurried kiss that lasted several miles, but still I knew it would end before I wanted it to. His hand moved to the back of my neck, and his lips moved against mine, silent but intense. I ran my fingers through his hair and then let them trail down his jaw and neck until my hand rested on his chest. I could feel his heart beating through his shirt.

Finally, his lips left mine. "I'm sorry," he whispered.

"What for?"

"For putting you in an embarrassing situation. You're always such a good sport."

I shook my head against his neck. "I ruined your teaching streak. I was hopeless."

"It's a good thing it doesn't matter if you can wakeboard or not."

I turned my head and kissed his jaw. He laced our

fingers together and rested his head against mine. I sighed. Soft music played as I fell asleep. Happy.

Chapter 10

I was sketching some ideas for a series of postcards for an old silver mine in Virginia City, Nevada when my phone rang. I glanced at the caller ID and saw it was Will.

"Hey, little brother. You ready for some good, live music?" "Little brother" was a long-standing joke between us because I was ten minutes older, and although he ended up several inches taller than me, there had been one year of awkward adolescence when I had him by almost two inches. Will had insisted we stand back to back almost daily so we'd know the moment he became taller than me. It was a ritual Mom grew to loathe.

Will sighed. "That's what I'm calling you about."

"Is something wrong?"

"Gina insisted I call you and tell you what I'm thinking."

I was confused. "Okay. What are you thinking?"

"I'm thinking I shouldn't go to the concert. Gina says I should go and take Angus with me, but I don't feel right about it."

"Gina can't go?"

"She's sick. Well, not sick, sick, but this pregnancy is beating her up. She can't keep anything down, not even water. We had to take her in for an IV twice last week just so she doesn't get too dehydrated. I appreciate the tickets, and I wish we could go, but I'd worry about her all night, and I don't want to leave her throwing up in the bathroom while I go to a concert."

"Will, I'm so proud of you. You're such a thoughtful husband. You make me feel like I raised you right.

"You're nuts."

"I'm only sorta joking. I totally understand, and I think that's thoughtful of you."

"You're not upset since you gave them to me?"

"If you were blowing it off to go watch cage fighting or something, I'd be bothered, but not if you're missing it to take care of your wife. Don't be silly."

"I was thinking of giving the tickets to Angus. He can take Wyatt, and then the tickets won't go to waste. And he could use a good distraction."

"Is something going on with Angus I don't know about?" Suddenly, I felt guilty. Since Kyle and I had been dating, I hadn't checked in much with Angus.

"He's trying to decide where to do his residency, and he has to decide soon."

"I assumed since he's still dating Wyatt, he'd choose Alameda."

"He likes Wyatt, but I'm not sure how much. It sounded like he might be leaning toward New York. He thinks he'd like it there, but I'm also wondering if he might be thinking the distance will let things end naturally without anyone getting hurt."

"Oh. He doesn't want to see if it can work out?" Sometimes Angus was such a puzzle.

"I've never understood him when it comes to dating. He dates great women but it never goes past a certain point.

Anyway, I know he's been trying to sort out his future, and I think the concert might be a nice distraction. As long as you don't care, since you gave me the tickets."

"Of course I don't care. I'd rather have them go to family than not get used."

"I thought you'd feel that way. I wish Gina felt better, so we could use them."

"I do too. Take good care of her, and tell her I love her. Is there anything I can do to help?"

"Nah. The doctor says it'll just take time. Thanks for being understanding."

It should have been warm. It was the end of June, after all. It rained for hours the day of the Mumford and Sons concert, and even though the rain stopped more than an hour before the concert started, the evening was chilly and damp. When Kyle and I arrived at America's Cup Pavilion, workers at the venue were drying off seats, and the coffee and hot chocolate lines were the longest in the tent.

I looked around the tent for Angus and Wyatt, sure Angus would want some hot cocoa with extra whipped cream, but I couldn't find them.

I was excited. I love live music and had been a Mumford and Sons fan since before they'd become so popular. Even though I felt bad Will and Gina weren't here, I was glad Angus was coming. He was the one who'd introduced me to their music, and I knew he'd like it.

We walked out of the tent and made our way to our seats. We were seated a few rows from the stage, a little to the right. People laughed and yelled around us, some already intoxicated. The fresh, just-after-rain smell was occasionally interrupted by the too-sweet scent of a few people smoking things security must have decided to ignore.

"Hey, guys, how's it going?" Angus and Wyatt stood at the end of our row. We moved into the aisle to talk.

I hugged Angus and Wyatt and took Kyle's arm, pulling him forward. "This is Kyle. Kyle this is my friend since forever, Angus, and this is his friend, Wyatt." After my conversation with Will, I was suddenly unsure how Angus would want Wyatt introduced.

Kyle shook their hands and then put his hand on my shoulder.

"I'm glad you guys were available to use the tickets," I said.

"I feel terrible for Will and Gina. She must be pretty miserable to miss this," Angus said.

I nodded. "Will said she's had to get fluids by IV since she can't keep anything down. Sounds awful."

"Some people have such a hard time with pregnancy," Wyatt said. "My older sister was really sick. Makes me nervous. Good thing babies are so cute or who'd want to risk it?"

"So you're an aunt?" I asked.

"I have two nephews. Totally worth the sickness." She snickered. "Easy for me to say, isn't it?"

We laughed. "Kyle's an uncle, too. Angus and I have to wait for Will and Gina's baby, and then we'll join you in the ranks of uncle and aunthood," I said.

"Honorary unclehood for me, but I'll take it," Angus said. His parents had always wanted to give him a brother or sister, but it had never happened. So he'd either have to marry someone with nieces and nephews or be satisfied being the honorary uncle to any kids born to the Emersons.

"I guess we'd better go find our seats." Angus pulled out the tickets.

"You're over there on the side in the ninth row." I

pointed at a section farther back. "Sorry about that. Will got me better tickets than I got him."

Angus gave me a chastising look and shook his head. "I think Will just took the lead."

"Hey, you're here, aren't you? That oughta be worth something."

"And Will gave me the tickets. Thanks for reminding me. He keeps moving up."

I punched Angus in the arm.

"We're going to get a bite to eat after the concert if you two would like to join us," Kyle said.

"Yeah, you should," I agreed.

Angus and Wyatt looked at each other, and Wyatt smiled and gave a little shrug.

"Sure, why not?" Angus said. "Where are you going?"

"Charlotte voted for breakfast food, so we thought we'd go to Happy Cakes."

"Sounds good. We'll meet you there after the show," Angus said.

We moved back to our seats and sat down, while Angus and Wyatt made their way to theirs.

"Will took the lead in what?" Kyle asked when we were seated.

"Ever since we were kids, he's teased us about which twin he likes best. He had a good thing going there for a while 'cause we both wanted to be the favorite, so we'd do nice things for him, and he'd pretend he was keeping a tally of who was the favorite. Then we got wise. Now it's an old joke."

"Smart guy." Kyle laughed. "I can't wait to meet Will so I can see which one of you is my favorite."

"Dang, I'm probably going to lose again," I said.

Kyle pulled me close and kissed me. "You're at a

definite advantage."

"I am?"

"Of course. You can rack up bonus points any time you want."

This time I kissed him. "Like this?"

"See, you're ahead already."

The concert was good. Kyle didn't recognize some of the songs, but he wasn't embarrassed at my cheering or singing along to almost everything. The biggest disappointment was the playlist didn't include a couple of my favorites. I kept waiting, but they didn't come. I was happy when they played Angus's favorite song during the second encore. I craned my neck and found Angus when it started. He gave me a long-distance high five.

It was nearly midnight by the time we got to Happy Cakes. Angus had texted to say they were almost there, so we sat on a red vinyl bench by the front door and waited for them. After the chill of the outdoor concert, the bright lights and warm interior of Happy Cakes felt almost tropical.

"It's so hot in here," Wyatt said when we were seated at a booth.

"There's a hook here at the end if you want to take off your jacket," Angus said. We all took off our jackets, and the guys hung them up. I suddenly felt frumpy in my jeans and loose-fitting sweater. Wyatt also wore jeans, but they had to be a couple sizes smaller than mine, and even though her crisp, white blouse wasn't skimpy, the fit and the two unclosed buttons made it unintentionally sexy. At least it appeared to be unintentional.

"Sorry they didn't play 'Winter Winds,' Chuck," Angus said.

"I know. I was bummed. I was afraid they weren't going to play 'White Blank Page.' Thank goodness they had two encores or you'd have been disappointed too."

"Chuck?" Kyle asked, grinning.

"Oh yeah. I forgot you'd never heard my lovely nicknames before."

"Kinda cute," Kyle said.

"No." I pointed at Kyle. "Don't start using it. And you." Now I pointed at Angus. "You've got to stop calling me that in front of new people. You were supposed to let that nickname die a long time ago."

"It's better than Chuckers," Angus said.

"Chuckers?" Kyle asked.

"That one's just mean." Wyatt gave me a look of solidarity. "I think you should call her Charlotte. If you feel the strange, adolescent urge to use a nickname, you should at least limit it to Charlie."

"Thank you," I said. "Listen to her, Angus. She's obviously a smart woman."

"There's no denying she's a smart woman," Angus said. "But I'm not sure she knows what she's talking about when it comes to nicknames. She's never had one."

"My name is Wyatt. There was no need for a nickname."

"That's kind of a great name," Kyle said.

"I like it fine now, but let me tell you, growing up was a nightmare. Kids at school had a heyday with it."

"Is it a family name?" I asked.

"I wish it were. Then there'd at least be a good reason for her to use it. My Mom always liked it, so since she wasn't having any more kids after me, she decided she'd have to use it on me or give up ever having a Wyatt. So she named her sweet baby girl Wyatt."

"What's your sister's name?" I asked.

"Penelope. To be honest, I think I prefer Wyatt, but

112

don't ever tell my sister. She thinks she was the lucky one."

Our food came, and we must have been starving because we all attacked our meals.

"Charlotte tells me you're starting your residency this fall," Kyle said to Angus.

"Just trying to decide where I want to be for the next few years." I noticed Angus didn't look at Wyatt.

"My vote is still Alameda," I said, "but it might be fun to come visit you in New York. How soon do you have to make a decision?"

"Soon," Angus put another bite of food in his mouth. I had the feeling he didn't want to talk about it anymore, so I helped him out. "Working on any exciting events?" I asked Wyatt. "She's an event planner," I told Kyle.

"I've got a huge wedding the day after tomorrow," Wyatt said. "I was glad the concert was tonight or I couldn't have come."

"She's also doing a big fund-raising dinner for Mercy House in a few weeks."

"What's Mercy House?" I asked.

"It's a shelter for kids whose parents are in jail or rehab," Wyatt said. "They're trying to help people learn about it. I was trying to get someone with a big name to attend, but so far the biggest name I have is Colletta Scott."

"Who?" Kyle asked.

"Exactly," Wyatt said. "Don't get me wrong. I'm happy she's on board, but she's not very well known. She had a minor role in Tom Cruise's sci-fi movie a few years ago, but I don't think many people know her by name."

"Would a political name help?" Kyle asked.

"Don't tease me," Wyatt said, and we laughed.

Kyle laughed. "I'm not teasing. I could check with Dad and see if he and Mom could attend. It'd be a win-win, right?

They get attention for helping a good cause, and it would help Mercy House get some good media coverage. If you want me to check with them, I can."

"Of course. That'd be great."

It was well after one when we finally left the booth and headed for the parking lot. "Thanks for getting Will the tickets," Angus said.

"No problem. Tonight was fun."

"Yeah, we should do it again sometime," Wyatt said.

"I'll be in touch about the fund raiser," Kyle said as we got in our separate cars.

We pulled up to my curb, and Kyle walked me to the gate. "I think I'll go to the fund raiser whether Dad can or not. It sounds like a good cause."

"Angus says Wyatt does a good job. It'd probably be a nice evening and a good meal."

"Want to come with me?"

"I'd love to."

"Let's plan on it. If my parents come, we can all go together. They think you're great."

"They're pretty great, too. It says a lot that they can like me even when I make a fool of myself."

"They were impressed with how hard you tried."

I groaned. "You'll have to teach me how to drive the boat. Then you can all do tricks, and I can make myself useful. Unless you're afraid I'd drag one of you to death. Or run over you. Maybe you shouldn't teach me to drive the boat after all. It's kind of a scary thought."

Kyle put his hands on my shoulders and smirked. "You don't scare me at all, Chuckers."

I took a step back and swatted his chest. "Don't call me that. That's the worst one of all and I hate it."

Kyle laughed.

"I'm serious."

"Don't worry. I like Charlotte better." He took my face in his hands and kissed me. His arms slid around my back and he pulled me closer, his lips never leaving mine. "I probably should have turned my car off," he finally said against my mouth. He let out a long breath and took a few steps backward, toward his car.

I unlocked my gate. "Have a good night," I turned to wave goodbye.

He stepped toward me and kissed me one more time before he walked to his car. "I'll call you tomorrow," he said over the top of the car. When I was safely inside, he got in and drove away.

Chapter 11

"And now you know the whole Jelly Belly story," Barney Berry Blue Jelly Belly said from the screen.

"This isn't the whole story," said Bubblegum Betty.

"What did we miss?" asked Barney Berry Blue.

"Eating them!" said Bubblegum Betty.

Barney Berry Blue laughed and turned toward the audience who sat on little benches in the screening room. "Of course. No Jelly Belly story would be complete without tasting us. Let's go through that door on the left, and you can sample our delicious flavors."

"And don't forget to mix and match us. My favorite combination is Toasted Marshmallow and Chocolate Pudding."

"That's pretty good, but my favorite is buttered popcorn and root beer. It's like a movie theater in your mouth."

"After you've found your favorites, be sure to stop at the Jelly Belly store and buy Jelly Bellys for you and all your friends."

"Thanks for visiting the Jelly Belly factory."

"Come back again."

The lights came up, and teachers and parents lined up a

first grade class to go sample the Jelly Bellys.

"It turned out great, Charlotte." Jasper Summers was the director who'd hired Fife to put together the Jelly Belly tour.

"This was a fun project. I'm glad you liked it. Seriously though, nothing like a room full of kids to make you nervous about the finished product. I was afraid they were going to hate it."

"They loved it. You had them at the Jelly Belly disco dance. That was a genius way to start. It's hilarious. If you ever need a recommendation, let me know."

"Thank you."

"Be sure to stop in at the store. Cheryl's got a gift basket for you."

Mom and I made our way around the two dozen first graders who were sampling different Jelly Belly flavors and into the factory store. "Jasper said to see you," I said to the cashier wearing the "Cheryl" nametag.

"Oh, you must be Charlotte. We put this together for you. Great tour, by the way."

Cheryl pulled out a large basket from a shelf beneath the cash register.

"Oh my. This is huge."

"It's got a bunch of the new Snapple flavors. You'll like those," Cheryl said.

"Thanks for inviting me," Mom said when we'd put the basket of Jelly Bellys in the back seat. "It's fun to see what you do."

"Thanks for coming with me. I wanted some moral support in case the kids started booing."

"That wasn't likely. I wish I could come with you this afternoon. Of course, the day you're going to help Gina ends up being the day I have an impossible-to-schedule doctor's appointment."

"Nothing serious, though, right?" I asked.

"No, just routine. It's just hard to get in to them. I've had this scheduled for more than a month."

"It'd be fun to have you come along, but don't worry. I figured since I was coming out here this morning, I'd take the rest of the day off and go help Gina get on top of things." The pregnancy was still keeping her down most of the time.

Mom was quiet, and when I glanced at her, she gave me a mischievous smile.

"What's that all about?" I asked.

"Angus told Will that you and Kyle really like each other." Her voice was silly and sing-songy.

I laughed. "Oh did he?"

"So are things progressing?"

"Yeah, I guess so. He's cooking me dinner tonight. Do you think that's a good sign?"

"It depends on how well he cooks," Mom said. "What does he do for a living?

"He works at his Dad's tech company. I don't know what it is exactly. Something complicated and techy. He's a great guy, and I like him a lot. Which makes this whole thing a little scary given my track record, you know."

"Knock it off. Your track record is just fine."

"Mom, you don't have to say that. I know you and Dad worry. You think Will and McKayla never talk?"

"We just want you to be happy," Mom said.

"I know. And if we're being honest, I've done my fair share of worrying. Did you know Hannah and some others—I'm not even sure who all it was—call me the husband maker?"

"Hannah Shelton? Mavis's daughter?"

"Yeah. My old roommate."

"I thought she was your friend." Momma Bear was suddenly appearing.

"She was. She still is, I think, even though we haven't seen each other for years now. I overheard Mrs. Shelton telling someone that at Harrison's wedding."

"That's awful. Why would they say something like that?"

"Because Mom. It's kinda true. Have you not noticed a pattern? Haven't you noticed every guy I've dated since high school has gotten married right after we quit dating?"

"I knew there were a couple. Harrison, of course. And Taz."

Taz. Mom probably remembered Taz because of his unforgettable name.

Taz was a musician who I'd met at the school. My graphic arts professor had a younger brother who was the drummer in a band called Soul Magnets. Taz wrote most of their music, played guitar, and sang. The band had arranged with our professor to have our class design a CD cover for the demo they'd be sending to radio stations and record producers around the country. I'd come up with the winning design. My reward was a photograph with the band in the department newsletter and tickets to a live show at The Sepia Underground.

The Soul Magnets were a pretty good band—a little darker and moodier than I was used to, but pleasant. After the show, Taz invited me to go get tacos. He was brooding and a little mysterious, and his smiles were rare and measured. Once, after we watched Lady Gaga win an award wearing a meat dress, I offered to make the band matching shirts made of tuna casserole. It wasn't that funny, really, but Taz was in a good mood that night, and he laughed. Aloud. Twice.

It was by far my proudest Taz moment.

We dated for a couple of months, and then Taz said he needed to talk to me. We sat in a backstage room that looked like the inside of a garbage can. Taz strummed unhappy minor chords and refused to look at me. Quietly, he told me my sunny disposition was a drain on his creative energies, and everything he'd written since we met had been crap. I wasn't inspiring his creativity.

Taz took a break from dating after that, which would explain the year that elapsed between our breakup and his wedding to a sad mime who performed at Fisherman's Wharf. He must have found her silence stimulating. Or maybe it was the black tear painted on her white face.

Taz still holds the record for longest stretch of time between our last date and marriage to the next girl.

I love him a little bit for that.

"Mom, it's been everyone. I've noticed the pattern. I just didn't know other people had until I heard what they call me."

"Mavis should sit Hannah down and teach her about kindness and manners."

I laughed. "She's a married woman now. It's a little late for a time out. But thanks for always looking out for me."

"It's been everyone? Are you sure?"

"I'm sure."

"Those boys were fools. There must be someone very special out there for you." Spoken like a true mother. "Maybe it will be Kyle."

A girl could hope. "Maybe so."

"Charlie, you don't have to do this," Gina said when she

answered the door. She looked pale and gaunt.

"I want to. I'm so sorry you've been so sick. Have you lost weight?" Gina didn't have a lot of weight she could afford to lose.

"I've lost eleven pounds since I got pregnant."

"Is that okay? Are the doctors worried?"

Gina rubbed her nearly flat stomach. "The doctor says this little guy is taking everything he needs. It's me that's going without."

"What a greedy little baby," I said.

"Seriously. We're going to have a talk about selfishness when he's born."

"Do you know it's a boy?" I asked.

"No. For some reason, I always say he or him. Probably because that's what Will does." She spoke to her stomach. "Sorry if you're a little girl."

"I hope this doesn't last much longer," I said.

Gina laughed weakly. "Me too. The biggest worry right now is keeping me from becoming dehydrated."

"Let's get you resting. I'm going to change your sheets and clean your bathroom and kitchen. You're going to either sleep or watch ridiculous daytime television while I'm here."

Gina hugged me. "I owe you."

"Remember that when you're looking for someone to watch your baby. Aunt Charlotte gets to be first."

"Do you want to stay for dinner? I can have Will pick up something on the way home."

"Maybe another time. Kyle's fixing Italian food for dinner tonight."

"Ooh, he's cooking for you. That's always a good sign. I knew I wanted to marry Will the night he cooked seafood chowder and biscuits." An unpleasant sound rumbled in Gina's throat, and tears sprang to her eyes. "I can't even talk about food without gagging."

"You poor thing. Go watch something good on TV, and I'll get started. Just don't put it on The Food Network."

The house was sparkling, and I was getting ready to leave when Will arrived home from work. "Charlie, you're an angel," he said.

"Yeah, I've been hearing that a lot lately," I said, remembering the embarrassing exchange with CJ in the grocery store.

"Gina says you have big dinner plans, so don't feel like you have to hang around since I just got here."

"Thanks." I hugged them both. "I love you guys."

I showered and dressed carefully for dinner. I wore a navy, cotton voile dress with embroidery and red, flat sandals. I still didn't know what I was going to wear to the Mercy House fundraiser. I fired off a text, asking Mia if she could shop with me on Saturday.

Within seconds, she'd agreed with three smiley faces and four exclamation points. She clearly liked shopping more than I did.

I took a taxi to Sacramento Street in Pacific Heights. Kyle's condo was on the top floor of an eleven story building. The yellow lobby with Victorian-style crown moldings and wainscot didn't prepare me for the modern interior of his condo. I was surrounded by dark wood, glass, leather and stone. It was a classic bachelor's home with nothing feminine in sight. The aroma of cooking food was wonderful.

"What smells so good?" I asked after Kyle kissed my cheek.

"Baked rigatoni with Italian sausage and peppers. It's almost finished."

"Good, 'cause I'm starving."

"I made plenty."

I followed Kyle into the kitchen—the spotless, white kitchen. There were white cabinets, white quartz countertops, and bright white lights."

"Did you really make dinner, or did you order in and dump it in a baking dish?"

Kyle clutched his heart. "Oh, no. Why would you doubt my abilities?"

"Because look at this kitchen. It's spotless. Is it possible to be this clean after cooking Italian?"

"All right. I shouldn't have to prove anything to you when you're showing so little faith in me, but come here." He took my hand and guided me to the stainless steel dishwasher where he motioned for me to open it. "Satisfied?" He grinned at me as I looked at the pots and pans and dishes inside.

"Please forgive me for doubting you. It's almost like you're trying to impress me or something."

"Is it working? Because that's exactly what I'm trying to do."

"Oh yeah. A man who cooks and cleans up after himself is pretty impressive."

"You'd better taste it before you get too carried away."

"If it tastes anything like it smells, then you're quite a catch."

Kyle pulled out a pan from the oven and carried it to a small dining room table. Two walls of windows surrounded the great room, where leather couches and chairs took up the bulk of the room, and the dining table took a smaller part. "This is beautiful." I walked to the window and looked out at the bay. The panoramic view took in The Golden Gate Bridge and Alcatraz Island. "I think you might have the best view in the city."

Kyle walked up behind me and put his arms around me. "The view is what sold this place. It's smaller than I wanted, but these windows more than made up for it. And it still has two bedrooms, so it's got a little room to grow."

Did that mean something, or was Kyle speaking hypothetically? Oh, I wanted it to mean something. Kyle was so close to perfection, and he liked me. I felt like I was on a roller coaster, climbing higher and higher. Was Kyle going to take me for the ride of my life, or was the car going to come off the tracks and crash to the ground in a pile of twisted wreckage? I hadn't felt this hopeful in a long, long time, and I'd discovered long ago that hope can keep you alive and feeling, but it also leaves you open and unprotected.

Kyle turned me to face him and kissed me. "Let's eat. I've got some exciting things I want to tell you about."

Either I was starving, because all I'd eaten since mid-morning was a small bag of Jelly Bellys, or Kyle was a world-class chef. It was probably a little of both.

We sat kitty-corner to each other so we both had a view of the city lights, as well as ourselves reflected against the dark windows. "So, you know my Dad's been a senator for sixteen years, right?" Kyle said as we finished up our meal.

"I knew it was a long time, but I didn't know how long."

"His term will end in not quite two years, and he's ready to do something else."

"Is he running for president?" I asked. I was mostly joking. The thought of knowing someone who could possibly be president seemed outrageous.

"No. Not president. I think he's considering running for governor, though. He thinks he could clean up the mess California's in. It wouldn't be for a few years though. If he didn't run for congress again, he'd finish up, and then he'd have two years until the governor's race. So it'd give him time to put the campaign together. He always said he'd never run for one elected office while he was serving in another elected office. He doesn't think that's fair to the people who sent him to do a job."

"That's very responsible of him. I've always wondered about senators who are supposed to be in Washington, but running all over the country campaigning for something else."

"Dad's a good man. The thing he's most worried about is leaving office with no good alternatives to replace him, so . . . " Kyle reached for my hand. " . . . that's where I come in."

I felt a tightening in my chest and a twisting in my stomach. Kyle was about to tell me something important, and suddenly I wasn't sure I wanted to hear it. "I'm going to run for the office he's vacating. We've been talking about it for years. I wasn't sure if Dad would be ready to move on after this term, or if he'd want to do one more, but he's decided if he wants to run for governor, now's the time to start thinking about that. The governor's ratings are terrible. Dad wants to capitalize on that. And I can capitalize on Dad's high ratings. He's got a lot of support, and he's sure he can send most of that support my way. Devon—that's his strategist—thinks I could keep most of Dad's base and bring in a lot of younger people."

I nodded, but I wasn't sure what I was nodding about. I just knew I needed to respond somehow, and nodding was all I could muster until I had a chance to take it all in.

"Charlotte, I can tell you're a little flustered."

"Maybe a little. Surprised, I mean. I didn't know you had political aspirations. I suppose I could have guessed. You're a political family, and you're a lot like your Dad. I just didn't know."

I stared at my hand. Kyle held it in both of his and traced circles around my knuckles with his thumbs. "I'm telling you this because I don't want you to hear it somewhere else." He dipped his head and dragged my eyes to his. "Dad and Mom are going to the Mercy House benefit. Devon thinks that would be a great setting to start putting myself front and center. Dad talked to Wyatt, and they've arranged for him to say a few words and then introduce me and have me say a few words. It'll start to get the media talking about me, and Devon can work in little appearances here and there over the next six months or so that will prepare everyone for me to announce I'm running for Dad's seat."

I needed to respond. So far I'd given him nothing, and he needed to know I was hearing him at the very least. "That's great. You'll do a fabulous job. At the benefit and as a senator, I'm sure."

"You're still going with me, right? To the benefit?"

"Of course."

"I can tell this is a lot to spring on you, and you need time for this to sink in. I'm telling you everything because . . ." Kyle slid his chair a little closer to mine and held my hand again. "I think you can probably tell I'm falling for you, Charlotte. And if this is going somewhere, which I think it is, this affects you as much as it does me." One of his hands moved up and down my arm. He let out a little laugh. "Are you okay? You look scared to death."

My stomach was a twisting and turning mess, but I didn't know if it was because this was going somewhere or because of the bomb Kyle had just dropped. I tried to laugh but it sounded like more of a squeak. "I'm fine. This is a lot to think about?"

"What are you thinking?" His hand continued to move

up and down my arm, and I found it comforting.

"Well, you've said a lot of things tonight. I guess my favorite is that you're falling for me."

Kyle laughed and kissed me. "I think that's my favorite part too. Please tell me you're okay with the rest. Mom's been telling me for weeks that I needed to fill you in, but I've been afraid I'd scare you away."

"I won't lie. It's pretty scary. I've never imagined anything like this. But if I'm being honest, I'm falling for you, too. So if this is part of the package, I guess I'd better get my head wrapped around it."

Kyle stood and pulled me into his arms. I wrapped my arms around his waist and held on. I needed to be strong and supportive, but right now I needed his strength and support. "You're amazing, Charlotte. I finally feel like I can breathe."

"Well, that makes one of us." I wasn't sure if I'd ever take a normal breath again.

Kyle hugged me, rocking gently back and forth. I could tell he was relieved and happy, so I boxed up my shock and fear and pushed it to the back of my mind. There would be plenty of time to pull it out and examine the change my life had taken tonight. For now, I'd be happy that Kyle was happy.

And he was falling for me.

Chapter 12

I had no idea what to wear to the Mercy House benefit. My ignorance was magnified by the knowledge that now I was dressing not just for a benefit, but for an event in which my date would be speaking and hinting at an upcoming political campaign.

Mia's style was fun and flirty, but I could tell by the first stop on Saturday that she wasn't equipped to help me dress for this sort of occasion.

"What about something like this?" she asked, holding up a hot pink babydoll dress that would hit her just above the knee, but would be scandalously short on me.

I shook my head. "First of all, you have to take my height into account. Secondly, I think I need to go pretty conservative. I'd rather not look like a cheap prostitute at my first fundraiser."

"Cheap prostitute worked for Julia Roberts."

"That was fiction." I sighed. "Oh Mia, how am I going to do this? I've never wanted people to notice me. I don't know if I can pull this off."

Mia waived me off like I was crazy. "You'll be fine."

"But he's going into politics. And we're not talking small, local stuff."

"He hasn't won anything yet," Mia said. "And he hasn't

asked you to marry him, so there's no guarantee this will affect you in any way." My face must have fallen the way my heart just had, because Mia instantly looked sorry and walked around the rack of clothes to hug me. "I wasn't meaning he wouldn't want to marry you. If he's smart, he will. I mean, don't worry so much about something that hasn't happened. Yet."

"You're right. But I feel like this might be different, and I know it doesn't even make sense, but it seems like I lost something, and I didn't even have it yet."

Mia looked confused. "Come again?"

I sighed. "Almost since we started dating, I've pictured how a future with Kyle would be. I pictured a nice house—"

"A very nice house," Mia interrupted, still browsing through the formal dresses.

"A husband with a secure and comfortable job—"

"Who makes a boatload of money."

I rolled my eyes. "And a normal family."

"Normal if the Kennedys are normal."

"You're not helping me," I said.

"Sorry." Mia didn't look sorry.

"Now I have to completely re-think that future. I have to imagine public appearances and standing behind Kyle while he gives speeches, and either moving my family clear across the country or staying here and being a single parent part of the year."

"Seriously, Charlotte, you're thinking way too hard. Just take it a day at a time. And if at any point, you don't want the future in front of you, leave."

"That's not even realistic. You don't just leave if you love someone."

Mia froze and looked at me over the rack. "You love Kyle?"

I turned away and started moving dresses around on a rack, even though I wasn't really looking at any of them. Suddenly, Mia's hand was on mine, stopping my hands from their pointless task. "You love him?"

I shrugged.

"Does he love you?"

"He hasn't said it, but I think he might."

"Well, that changes everything."

"I know. That's what I'm trying to tell you. I'm falling in love with Kyle, and I saw a future I liked. Then he cooks me delicious food and drops a bomb that completely changes everything. And it scares me. I'm not sure I like this alternate universe. And I'm not sure I'll be any good at it."

"Kyle must think you'll be fine. If he's known this was the path he was going to take, don't you think he'd have stopped dating you if he didn't think you could handle it? Give yourself some credit."

I sighed. "Look at me. I don't even know what to wear to a stupid party. And no offense, but you're proving to be no help at all."

"This is definitely not my area of expertise." Mia held up another dress. "Hot little numbers for a night on the town? That I can handle. I know how to dress you so a guy can't take his eyes off you, but I'm not sure what you should wear if the eyes of the world are going to be on you."

I groaned.

"Call his mom. You said she was nice. Call her. Ask her what you should wear. She's been doing this for a long time. It would probably make her feel good to know you were seeking out her help."

Mia surprised me. She'd never been particularly good at admitting her own weaknesses—not that being unsure what I should wear to a benefit was actually a weakness—but even more than that, she was making a pretty calculated suggestion. I was used to Mia flying by the seat of her pants.

I texted Kyle and within minutes had Roberta's phone number. We found a little couch by one of the dressing rooms. "What do I say?"

"Ask her what you should wear."

My hands shook as I dialed her number.

"Hello. Is this Roberta?"

"Yes."

"Hi. This is Charlotte."

"How are you, dear?" Her voice was loaded with concern.

"I'm fine." I sighed. "I think. I'm not sure what kind of dress I should be looking for. For the benefit, I mean."

"Of course. So you're going to come?"

"Yes."

"I'm glad. And did Kyle talk to you about his plans?"

"Yes."

There was an awkward pause. "Charlotte, are you shopping right now?"

"Yes, with my roommate."

"Would she mind if I joined you?"

Suddenly, I felt like crying. "I don't think she'd mind." I turned to Mia. "Do you mind if she comes shopping with us?"

Mia shook her head.

"She doesn't mind. We're at Union Square."

"I can be there in half an hour. Let's meet at Neiman Marcus. By the makeup counter."

"Thank you, Roberta."

"This will be fun. It'll give us a chance to talk."

Mia walked with me to Neiman Marcus. When we arrived at the makeup counter, she hugged me. "I'm going to take off."

"No way. You said you didn't mind if she joined us.

That means you're going to stay."

"Charlie, this woman could be your mother-in-law."

"And you're my friend."

Mia held up her hand. "This woman has also lived the future you're worried about. Talk to her. Ask her questions. Listen to her answers and listen to what she says behind her answers. Maybe this will help you not be so nervous."

"I was excited to shop with you."

"We'll shop when you need a new swimsuit or something to wear to your work Christmas party. She's the right one to help you shop for something like a benefit. I've never been to one of those in my life. What do I know?" I bit my bottom lip, and Mia laughed. "Stop worrying. Find something gorgeous."

"What if I can't afford what she thinks I should get?"

"Don't be cheap. Remember, if this continues, Kyle will be buying your expensive dresses. You can always look at this as an investment in your future life—the life where money won't be a concern at all."

"Is there such a world?"

"Learning how to spend money is probably going to be a bigger adjustment than any of the other things you're worried about. If Kyle's mom finds you the perfect dress, get it. Now, I'm going to go before she gets here."

Everything about Roberta was intimidating. Everything except her smile and her warm personality. She looked elegant in navy cigarette pants, a coral and white striped sweater set and pewter flats. Her blond hair was pulled up in an elegant twist, and she carried a gray, moderately-sized designer bag. I felt like an ogre standing next to her when she arrived. My hair was in a messy braid that hung over one shoulder, I'd worn almost no makeup, and my yoga pants and t-shirt had been intentionally chosen to make trying on dresses easy. Now that I was shopping with Roberta, I looked like the ugly step-daughter in desperate need of a makeover.

If Roberta noticed my dreadful appearance, she didn't let on.

"I'm so glad you called," she said. "I was facing an entire afternoon of listening to Donald and Devon strategize. This is much more fun." She put her arm through mine and guided me to the escalator. "I'm not sure if we'll find what you want here, but I figured it was a good place to start. Where's your friend?"

"She had some things to do and figured I was in good hands with you."

"Well, let's go prove her right. We'll start here, and if we can't find something appropriate, we'll widen our search."

Roberta had picked out three dresses within five minutes of arriving in the evening gown department, and already I could tell this was going to go better than the stop with Mia. "When you're looking for a dress you'll be wearing to an event like this, you want something elegant and conservative. You don't want it to draw too much attention, but you want it to be beautiful enough that those who do notice you are impressed. Daytime events are the same. You want something polished and professional, but also pretty. And you want it to look expensive without looking too expensive."

"Sounds terrifying," I said.

"It was the first few times I had to choose what to wear, but soon it became second nature."

After I'd tried on the dresses Roberta had chosen, she folded her arms and thought for a moment. "You know, I think you want something a little younger. These look more like my generation. If we're going to be appealing to a younger demographic, we want you to look conservative and elegant, but we also want you to dress your age. Let's check out a couple of other places."

Two hours later, I carried a dress bag out of Anthropologie. I'd never spent so much on clothing before, and I cringed at the hit my bank account had just taken. I had to admit, though, the dress and shoes were perfect.

"Do you have time to grab a sandwich at The Rotunda?"

I had no idea where The Rotunda was, but since I wasn't in a hurry, and I was actually quite hungry, I agreed. We walked back to Neiman Marcus and made our way to the posh, expensive restaurant where we ordered chicken salad sandwiches and raspberry lemonade.

"I'm so glad Kyle talked to you. And I'm glad it didn't send you running for the hills."

"I was surprised. I had no idea he had political aspirations."

"It's such a predicament since he's not married yet. Of course, he doesn't want to scare women off by telling them too much too soon, but at the same time, when I could tell he was interested in you, I felt it was important for you to know."

I wasn't sure what to say. This was Kyle's mother. Of course she'd have his best interests in mind and would want me to do whatever was best for Kyle. On the other hand, she was a woman who had lived the life that now might face me. Would she be honest with me?

"Charlotte, I can tell you've got a lot on your mind. Do you have any questions?"

I took a sip of water. "How did you do it? Did you move to Washington part of the year?"

"I stayed here and kept the boys in school the first few years. We thought the continuity was important. Each option has its pros and cons, but since Kyle and Peter were both in high school and were so involved, we figured it would be better for them. Shawn was already in college, so it didn't affect him as much. Alex had never been as involved in school, so when Peter graduated from high school, we decided we'd go to Washington with Donald. That meant we dragged Alex back and forth all through his high school years. I don't know that we did the right thing for him. I don't think he's ever felt settled. I've wondered if that's part of the reason he's always . . ." Her voice trailed off. "Well, anyway, I think it was hard on him."

"It's strange to be having this conversation. I mean, we're just dating."

"That's true. And it will be up to you two where you go with this. But I think you both need to know what lies ahead. You certainly do so you can decide if a public life is something you can live with. And of course, Kyle needs to know if you can fit into the future he's planned."

Roberta reached across the table and patted my arm. "I don't mean to sound heartless or harsh. It's just good to have all the information."

I nodded. Our sandwiches arrived, and the conversation turned to topics I had answers for, as Roberta asked about my job and we talked about our families. I learned that Donald and Roberta had met working on a campaign during a presidential election in the seventies. She told me Kyle was the only one of their four sons who had an interest in politics. Lucky for me!

Roberta paid our tab, and on the sidewalk in front of the store, she hugged me. "Don't ever hesitate to call me if you have any questions or worries." I was glad Mia had told me to call her.

Chapter 13

*D*ressing for the Mercy House benefit calmed my nerves. It was difficult to put on the orange blossom, Grecian style dress without feeling elegant and sophisticated. Because of my height, the bow-embellished, ivory flats looked pretty as they peeked out from under the dress. Thankfully, they were also comfortable. I styled my hair in smooth, loose curls with one side pulled back.

"You look amazing," Mia said when I walked into our little living room. I twirled, and the fabric floated around me.

"That's a red carpet dress," Graham agreed.

I took a deep breath and held it.

"I know this is all new to you," Mia said, "but try to have fun. Remember, it's for a good cause."

The doorbell buzzed, and Mia looked over the back of the couch. "It's him."

"I'm on my way," I said into the intercom.

"Mom said you were going to blow me away." Kyle said when I arrived downstairs. He took my hand and stepped back, looking at me with appreciative eyes. "She was right. You're stunning."

"Woowee!" Cuddy said from the doorway of the

barbershop. "Wish I was about forty years younger."

"Oh, Cuddy. No wonder I love you."

"You'd have to fight me for her," Kyle said.

"Forty years ago, I could have given you a run for your money." Cuddy winked at me.

The benefit was held at the Julia Morgan Ballroom. I'd never been there before and was awed by the beauty. Floor to ceiling arched windows lined the walls. Mahogany octagons covered the ceiling, giving it a honeycomb look, and an enormous fireplace took up nearly an entire wall. Large, round tables filled the floor. A riser with a podium stood in front of three of the windows. Each table had three framed pictures of children with the stories of what Mercy House had done to help them. Votives and short, crystal bowls with floating flowers surrounded the pictures, making the tables look stylish without detracting from the beauty of the children's faces.

I saw Wyatt from across the room, and she waved. She looked stunning in a navy, boat-necked dress with a beaded bodice and flowing, chiffon skirt. Her fiery red hair was tucked up in a neat chignon. Angus was right. She was gorgeous.

"How are you two doing?" Wyatt asked. Up close, she was even more beautiful. I could see the tiny headset she was wearing.

"We're great," Kyle said. "Just looking to see if Dad's here. Ah, there he is. Would you two excuse me for a minute?" Kyle squeezed my hand and left me to talk to Wyatt.

"Wyatt, this place is beautiful." I looked around the room.

"We're so lucky. They usually charge a huge event fee, but they're not charging Mercy House a thing. Someone on the board has a relative who has done volunteer work for Mercy House in the past. They pulled some strings, and when I called, they agreed to donate the ballroom. I was thrilled."

"The table decorations are perfect. Did you come up with that?"

Wyatt shrugged. "They weren't a big deal. I do things like this all the time. I love your dress, by the way. You look amazing."

"Thank you. I don't usually attend things like this, so I had to go shopping."

"You shopped well. Love the color."

"Do you always have to dress up for these things?" I asked. Wyatt looked like she'd stepped off the pages of a fashion magazine.

"It depends on the event. I dress up for weddings and formal evening events, but it's often more casual. This dress wouldn't work well at a corporate picnic. But I probably have more formals than the average girl. I should have had you come check out my closet. I might have something you could have worn, although you probably won't mind having that gorgeous dress hanging in your closet. Maybe I'll be calling you."

I laughed. "You're being kind."

"I'm not. I love it. By the way"—she leaned in and spoke quietly—"I wanted to thank you for introducing me to Kyle. Having his parents involved in this benefit was a huge score. Once they put out the word that they were attending, we sold almost a hundred more tickets. That's almost $50,000 more for Mercy House. And that doesn't even count any of tonight's donations. They were so happy."

"I think it was a win win. Kyle's family is getting some good exposure tonight, too."

"Well, thank you. I put you two and Kyle's parents at different tables. They're both near the front. Senator Aldsworth said he'd like Kyle to be seated with any media, and since you're with Kyle—"

"What are you two whispering about?" Kyle asked, putting his arm around my waist.

"You know. Dresses and table settings," I said.

Wyatt put her hand to her earpiece. "Thanks, Jeff. I'll be right there." Then she spoke to us. "If you'll excuse me, I've got to run to the kitchen. Have a wonderful evening. Maybe I'll catch up with you later." Wyatt moved gracefully toward the back of the room, pausing for a moment to straighten a table setting on her way.

"Everything good?" Kyle asked.

"Everything's great," I said.

"You're definitely the belle of the ball," he said and kissed my cheek. I laughed as I looked around the room at the beautiful dresses and tuxedoes. I wasn't sure I'd agree with 'belle of the ball.' I was glad I'd found a dress that fit in with all the finery. "Come say hi to Mom and Dad."

We moved through the tables, Kyle's hand on my back, to where Donald and Roberta were talking to a small group of people. Roberta looked sophisticated in a gray silk skirt and jacket. "Charlotte, it's great to see you," Donald said, kissing my cheek. "Edward and Beth, this is Kyle's girlfriend, Charlotte."

Edward and Beth expressed their delight to meet me, and Beth kissed the air beside my cheek.

"Don't you worry." Roberta linked her arm through mine and leaned close. "Relax and be yourself."

"Thank you. And thank you again for helping me find this dress."

"It was fun. Call me anytime."

139

After a few minutes, a tinkling bell chimed, and we made our way to the table with our place cards. An older woman stood at the podium and welcomed everyone to the benefit. "We're so happy to be here tonight for a wonderful cause. Mercy House has been helping children for almost forty years through generous donations from good people like you." She held her arms out to the audience, and polite clapping followed. "We're so honored to have some distinguished guests and contributors here this evening. We'll hear from them later. Mayor Jackie Pinelli and her husband, John." A couple seated at the same table as Donald and Roberta stood and waved to the crowd. "Senator Donald Aldsworth and his wife, Roberta." Donald and Roberta stood and waved. "And finally, Senator Aldsworth's son, Kyle, and his lovely date, Charlotte." My stomach dropped. Kyle took my hand, and we stood and waved. I felt like an awkward child playing dress up.

Kyle didn't let go of my hand when we sat back down. I was embarrassed that it was trembling. What was wrong with me? I'd stood in front of people before, hadn't I? My mind combed through the years, trying to remember a time when I'd had to stand before a large group of people, and finally, I had to admit that except for oral presentations in high school and college, I didn't have anything that had prepared me for this kind of attention. Suddenly, I wished I'd taken a speech class or my mom had entered me in pageants. Maybe then my hand wouldn't feel embarrassingly slick.

"Enjoy your dinner," the woman said and left the podium.

Dinner was delicious and fancy. Now I knew what a $500 per plate fundraiser got you. The room hummed with conversation. A couple sitting to Kyle's left immediately engaged him in conversation about the most recent session of congress and their take on the lagging economy. They included me by asking a couple of questions, but it was difficult to hear, and after I'd repeated my answers twice, they weren't in a hurry to ask me a third.

"So you're Kyle Aldsworth's date," said a woman to my right. She looked about thirty and had an intense gaze that seemed to pick up everything going on around us.

"Yes, I'm Charlotte. And you're . . ." I glanced at her place card. "Angela?"

"Yes. Angela Prescott." She shook my hand with the tips of her fingers. "It's a pleasure to meet you. I have to tell you, your dress blew me away when I walked in here. It's the most amazing dress in the room."

"Thank you."

"And there are a lot of beautiful dresses in the room, but yours is . . . Wow." Angela took a bite of her grilled vegetables. "Aren't you the girl who was injured in the hot air balloon accident a couple of months ago?"

I laughed. "That was me."

"That must have been terrifying for you. How are you?"

"It was pretty scary, but I'm doing fine."

"I saw the news story about the accident, and I instantly crossed that off my bucket list. I'd be too scared to try it now."

"Yeah, I don't think I'll be going up again anytime soon."

"It's so good of you to support a benefit like this," Angela said. "It's great for Mercy House to get extra exposure and to see politicians supporting things like this. Did you know Mercy House is a private organization? They don't get any government aid, which makes them a little less important to most of the politicians."

"I didn't realize that, but I learned some impressive

141

things about Mercy House when I started reading about it. I figured I should know as much as I could since I was going to be here tonight. I was impressed. Did you know Celeste Mendez lived at Mercy House while her father was in prison? Her mother had passed away, and she said Mercy House was a lifeline."

"I thought she might be here tonight, but I haven't seen her." Angela craned her neck and looked around the room.

"Probably on tour. I read she replaced all the old beds about a year ago." I was glad I'd done some reading so I had something to say.

"I like to hear about celebrities who don't forget where they came from."

I glanced at Kyle, who was still talking to the couple. He looked at me and winked. I wasn't sure, but it sounded like they were now talking about domestic terrorism. I was grateful Angela was so talkative. It kept me from looking awkward while Kyle schmoozed with what looked like important people.

"These poor kids have it pretty tough," Angela said.

I buttered a warm dinner roll. "I know. The stories of some of these sweet children broke my heart," I admitted. "It made me realize how lucky I am I never had to worry about where my next meal was coming from or what condition I'd find my mom in when I came home from school."

"I know. Can you imagine coming home to find your mom stoned or passed out?" Angela said. Across the room, Wyatt was directing three members of the wait staff toward a table in the middle. Angela leaned toward me. "I think we can all agree with that. Children should be playing with friends and going to the park, not cleaning up their mother's vomit."

Angela's tone and use of the word "vomit" startled me.

"It's sad to think these children are suffering, and none of it is their fault. It makes me glad there are places like Mercy House."

"Addiction is such a selfish thing. It's abuse if you ask me," Angela said and leaned to the side so a waiter could remove her plate. "So, tell me about this." She motioned back and forth between Kyle and me. "You two make a gorgeous couple."

"He's a pretty great guy."

Angela leaned toward me and lowered her voice. "Is it true you're secretly engaged?"

I wouldn't mind if that were true. "No. We're just dating."

"He must like you a lot to be making public appearances like this with you." I smiled and speared my last roasted red potato. "Have you met the family?"

"Most of them. They're really nice people."

"Have you met his brothers?"

"All but one."

"They're quite the family."

One waiter took my plate, and another placed a slice of chocolate cheesecake with berries in front of us. Angela pushed the berries aside and took a bite of the cheesecake. "This is why I volunteer for assignments like this. The food is almost always fantastic."

I ate my dessert, as well. I'd have liked to take Angela's berries off her hands since she didn't want them, but I knew that wouldn't make the best impression. "Would it be wrong to ask for seconds on this?" I asked, and Angela nodded.

"Have you met the youngest brother?" Angela asked between bites of dessert.

"Alex?" Angela nodded. "Yes, I've met him."

"Having a son arrested for a DUI must be extra hard for

a family in the public eye. Does he seem like the black sheep of the family?"

Thankfully, I didn't have a chance to answer. "We're so happy to hear from our special guests tonight." The woman who had spoken earlier was back at the mic. "First, we'll hear from Mayor Pinelli, then Senator Aldsworth, and then his son, rising star, Kyle Aldsworth. Mayor Pinelli."

"I'm here with a rising star," I whispered in Kyle's ear, and he put his arm on the back of my chair.

The audience clapped, and the mayor took the stage, thanking Mercy House for the wonderful work they were doing and thanking the guests for generously giving to the worthy cause.

Next was Donald. "It's a pleasure to be with you tonight. I was thrilled to get the invitation to attend tonight's benefit and to be in the presence of so many of you good citizens of the bay area. Places like Mercy House deserve our attention and our generosity. Too often in today's world, we see charities that ask for your money and promise you it's going to a good cause, only to discover later that questions have arisen as to the validity of the charity and concerns have been raised about how much of the money actually makes it into the hands of those who need it.

"The beautiful thing about Mercy House is the money you give tonight goes to the children who are being cared for there. It isn't going into the hands of a few greedy people. Catherine Merchant saw to that when she started it, and today it remains one of the shining examples of what can be done when people truly sacrifice for the good of others.

"I'm especially honored tonight to be joined by my good son, Kyle. Kyle is one of those sons every father hopes for, a son who works hard and makes something of himself. Kyle has become a man I'm proud of. He's a man of honesty and integrity, and a man who stands up for those in need. When you're a senator, there are many occasions and events where people introduce you and extoll your virtues. Sometimes it's downright embarrassing. But I'd be lying if I said I wasn't honored and proud to be able to introduce my son, Kyle Aldsworth."

Donald stepped back from the microphone as Kyle walked up to the podium. They shook hands, and Donald patted Kyle on the shoulder. Then he returned to his seat, and Kyle began to speak.

"Many years ago, Catherine Merchant opened her home to three children whose parents had been ordered by the court to get medical help to overcome their drug and alcohol addictions. Catherine wasn't a wealthy woman, but she had room in her home and love in her heart. It wasn't long before she realized those three children she was helping were just a small percentage of those that needed the same kind of help. So she went out into the community and gathered together others who recognized the need and were willing to help.

"Within two years, she'd approached enough people that she was able to sell her home and buy the building that is now Mercy House. Over the years, hundreds of children have been saved by Catherine Merchant's dream. Volunteers at Mercy House see to it that these children are fed, clothed and loved. They even help them with their homework.

"The bay area is a better place because of the work and love Mercy House offers, and I'm honored to donate today, on behalf of my family, a check for $30,000. I'd encourage all of you to open your hearts to these children and give generously."

The room filled with applause as people stood and cheered the generous donation.

"I heard Kyle is being groomed to run for his father's

seat in the senate." Angela was standing right beside me, her elbow bumping into mine as she clapped. "Is that true?"

I wasn't sure what to say. Did the Aldsworths and Devon want people to know yet? I kept my eyes on Kyle.

"Charlotte?" Angela prodded.

"Isn't he handsome?" I said as Kyle walked off the stage. Out of the corner of my eye, I saw Angela shaking her head.

Isn't he handsome? That's what I'd come up with to deflect her questions? I hoped I didn't look as embarrassed as I felt.

"You okay?" Kyle whispered in my ear when we were seated again.

I nodded and hoped no one else had heard my ridiculous comment.

"Tonight went well, I think," Kyle said on the drive home.

"Your speech was great. You got people excited. Wyatt said so far there's been more than $100,000 donated."

"It's nice to help out a good cause. Wyatt's good at what she does. I told Dad he ought to have her plan some of his events."

"It looked like a stressful job. I don't think she got to sit down for even a minute all night."

Kyle reached for my hand. "I hope you didn't feel neglected. The couple I was talking to are pretty important in the party, and they were talking my ear off."

"It was fine. I had a nice visit, too."

"I didn't recognize her."

"Her name is Angela. She was talkative, so it was pretty easy."

"You look so beautiful tonight. I was proud to have you there with me." He kissed my fingers and then laced his through mine.

"I was proud to be there with you."

"I know all this is a lot to deal with, but I think tonight proved you're up to the challenge."

"I hope so." I let out a long breath and leaned my head back against the seat. "Want to come up for a little while?" I asked.

"Yeah. After tonight, we've earned a little time to chill."

Kyle parked the car in the closest spot he could find, which was more than two blocks from my apartment. He'd offered to drop me off first, but I said I could walk. The air was warm, and we held hands. The door to Shanghai Kelly's was open, and we laughed at a particularly bad karaoke version of "I Will Survive."

The lamp was on when we reached the apartment, and Mia's door was closed. I kicked off my shoes, and Kyle laid his jacket across the back of a chair and took off his tie. I got a couple of bottled waters from the fridge while Kyle flipped through the channels, looking for something to watch. "I think we'll avoid any news channels. You want to watch *Antiques Roadshow*?" he asked.

I sat down beside him and tucked my legs up under me. "Sure," I said as he wrapped his arm around me.

"And by watch, I mean, do you want to listen to *Antiques Roadshow*?" He put down the remote and turned to face me. His mouth was warm and insistent when he kissed me, his arms pulling me closer.

At some point, *Antiques Roadshow* became *Austin City Limits,* but we didn't care. Sometime during *Austin City Limits*, Kyle told me he loved me. When *Austin City Limits* turned into a documentary about black widows, Kyle laughed and said that was his cue to leave. I walked him to the door.

"I'll call you tomorrow."

"I'll be here."

I turned off my alarm. It was late, and with a Saturday free of plans, I intended to sleep in as long as possible.

Chapter 14

Mia knocked on the door and opened it a crack. "I'm okay. I'm just sleeping in," I said, hoping she'd leave so I could get a couple more hours.

"Your cell phone has rung twice. I didn't recognize the number. Do you want me to turn it off?"

"What time is it?"

"It's not quite eight."

"Are you up because of my phone?"

"No. We're driving down to San Louis Obisbo for the arts and crafts show."

"I'll just turn the ringer off," I said.

Mia stepped into the room to hand me my phone. It had barely exchanged hands when it signaled I had a voicemail. I'd had less than six hours of sleep. I could listen to the voicemail later.

"Have fun down there," I said.

"I want a full report of the benefit when I get back." Mia stepped out of the room.

"It was great."

Mia giggled. "I'm sure it was."

I heard Mia close the door to the apartment as she left,

and I snuggled under my blanket. I hadn't fallen back asleep when my phone vibrated on the nightstand. Without lifting my head, I picked up the phone and looked at the display. There was a text from Kyle. Maybe he wanted to tell me he loved me again. I smiled as I hit the message button.

Kyle: Charlotte, you're not picking up. Please call me asap. It's urgent.

I scrolled through the incoming calls. Was the number I hadn't recognized Kyle?"

Me: Should I call your cell phone?

Kyle: Oh good. I'll call you back. Please pick up.

I sat up in bed and adjusted the pillows behind my back. What could be urgent? I hoped no one was sick or hurt.

"Hello," I answered on the first ring.

"Hey, Charlotte. We're in crisis mode, and we've got to talk to you right away. Before you talk to anyone else."

"What's wrong, Kyle?"

"It's about last night. An editorial appeared in the paper this morning, and it's blowing up. Can I come pick you up? We need to get your side of the story, and we probably need to make a statement this morning. I'm heading over to Dad and Mom's and can swing by and get you."

My head was spinning, and I couldn't get a deep breath. My voice cracked when I spoke. "My side? My side of what?"

"I'll tell you about it when I get there. Be ready in ten minutes. I'm already on my way. I've got to call Dad and Devon and let them know I reached you. See you soon."

I untangled my feet from the blankets and sat on the edge of the bed. What did I need to do to be ready in ten minutes? I pulled on a pair of sweat pants, a hoodie, and my flip flops before I headed to the bathroom. The sleek, smooth waves from the night before had mutated into a tangled nest. Running a brush through my hair proved to be impossible, so I pulled it back into a messy bun. My face looked awful. This should teach me to wash my face before I go to bed. I scrubbed off the previous night's makeup, wishing I had time to apply at least a coat of mascara, but the intercom was already buzzing as I dried my face. So much for makeup.

"I'm on my way down."

When I reached the sidewalk, Kyle was already in the car, waiting at the curb.

I had no idea what was going on, but the urgency in Kyle's voice had caused me concern. Now that he was waiting for me in the car—no greeting at the door, no kiss or casual conversation, no opening the car door for me—I was panicking.

Kyle put the car in gear and pulled away from the curb as soon as I'd shut my door. I quickly put on my seatbelt, then turned to Kyle.

"You said there's something in the paper?" I asked. I couldn't imagine what the problem could be. Last night had been a perfect night. Kyle's speech had been inspired. The benefit had gone off without a hitch. I hadn't fallen on my face or made a fool of myself. So what could possibly be happening? My heart was pounding so hard in my ears, I was afraid I wouldn't be able to hear Kyle's response.

"You're quoted in the paper. It doesn't sound good." Kyle was focused on the traffic, weaving in and out of cars as he headed toward his parents' house.

"I'm quoted? I didn't talk to many people last night."

"You talked to enough." His voice was unexpectedly brusque. He must have realized how he'd sounded because he glanced over at me and then patted my clenched hands. "I'm sorry. We'll get this all worked out." He put his attention back on the road and his hand back on the wheel. I took a deep breath and blinked back the tears that suddenly blurred everything in front of me.

It took us almost twenty minutes to get to the Aldsworths' house. It was a meticulously maintained, cream-colored Victorian set between a modern, wood and glass home and a slightly less perfect Victorian in three shades of blue. Kyle parked in an empty spot across the street, expertly fitting the car into the parallel spot on his first try. I'd have complimented him, but I was too nervous, and I could tell he didn't really care about his parking skills at the moment.

I didn't wait for him to get my door. I met him at the back of the car. He grabbed my hand with one of his and pushed a button on his key ring with the other. His car horn gave a short honk, and we darted across the road.

Roberta met us at the door, and her appearance confirmed this was serious. Her hair was pulled back in a severe ponytail at the nape of her neck. Her makeup-free face was lined with worry, and she looked older. She wore a pale green workout suit, and her feet were bare. "I'm so glad you reached her. Your father and Devon are in the office." She turned to lead the way, then apparently remembered I was there. She slowed and linked her arm through mine. "Good morning, Charlotte."

With Kyle holding my right hand and Roberta's arm through mine, I should have felt ready to face anything, but all I wanted to do was turn and run. Something was wrong, and somehow I was involved, even though I had no idea how.

The office was huge. A large window at the back end made everything and everyone inside the room look like dark silhouettes. At first, I thought Donald was sitting at his desk, but as we stepped closer, I realized he was standing by a fireplace, his arm resting on the mantle. I didn't recognize the man at the desk.

Roberta motioned for us to sit on a leather sofa that faced the fireplace, and the man at the desk came to join us. He dropped a newspaper onto the coffee table in front of us. "We've got to go through this line by line and figure out what is fact, what is fiction, and what is just exaggerated. Kyle leaned forward, his elbows on his knees, and looked at the newspaper. I was curious, but afraid to look.

"Devon," Roberta said. "I realize this is serious, but can we please have some manners? Charlotte, this is Devon Kemp, Donald's campaign strategist."

"And clean up man." Devon's voice held no humor.

"Devon, this is Charlotte. Let's bring Kyle and Charlotte up to speed without making them feel like they're the enemy here."

"Sorry, Roberta. Nice to meet you, Charlotte." Devon shook my sweaty hand, and then when I clasped my hands together again on my lap, Kyle slid his hands between mine and pulled my hand onto his lap.

Finally, my curiosity got the best of me, and I leaned forward to get a better look at the paper. The headline read "Is This the Change We Want?" A photograph of Kyle and me leaving The Julia Morgan Ballroom accompanied the article.

"Have either of you read the article?" Donald asked.

I shook my head.

"I pulled it up online and read it before I came," Kyle said.

"Then you can see we probably need to make a statement."

"Kyle, why don't you read it aloud? Charlotte needs to know what it says."

Kyle let go of my hand and picked up the paper. I wiped my hands on my sweat pants.

"'Is This the Change We Want' by Angela Prescott." It took me a moment to place where I knew that name. Then I recalled her dark hair and piercing eyes, and I remembered talking to her throughout dinner. My stomach clenched, and I was grateful I hadn't eaten breakfast. Kyle continued reading.

Last night was The Mercy House fundraiser at The Julia Morgan Ballroom. It was a beautifully pretentious evening of wealthy people eating expensive food and hobnobbing with other wealthy people. In their defense, they raised over a hundred thousand dollars for a worthwhile cause. But how many more children could Mercy House have cared for if the tens of thousands of dollars that were spent on food, tuxedoes, the venue, and the Oscar-worthy dresses worn by nearly every woman in attendance, had been donated to the cause?

But I digress. If the rich and famous want to see and be seen in order to be generous, we can indulge them that. The subject I'd like to talk about is the future of the senate seat currently held by Donald Aldsworth. For months now, there have been whispered rumors in political circles that Senator Aldsworth will be retiring after his current term ends. Other rumors, not so whispered, have hinted he would throw his considerable political clout behind his son, Kyle, a third-generation Aldsworth, who appears to have inherited his father's political aspirations. This would make sense. Like the Kennedys and the Bushes, politics run through their veins—Donald's father, James Aldsworth, was a Congressman in the 1960s.

By almost every measure, Kyle fits the bill. He's wealthy (of course), he's movie star handsome, and he's bright. The only real problem? He's single. Certainly not a deal-breaker for the people of Northern California, but as Roberta Aldsworth has demonstrated over the years, having a smart, attractive, well-spoken spouse is a proven asset. For almost two decades, whenever the Senator's numbers have taken a dip, all he's had to do is send out Roberta to make a speech here or a donation there, and his numbers have gone up. Crisis averted.

So it was with great interest that I sat beside Charlotte Emerson, the woman Kyle is dating and that the Aldsworths are grooming (if shopping trips and styling tips are any indication) to be the wife for the future Senator Kyle Aldsworth.

Kyle turned to me, his face tortured. "I'm sorry, Charlotte. This is awful."

I shook my head and whispered, "It's okay. Go ahead." I didn't really want him to go ahead. I wanted to rewind my day, go back to bed, and wake up with the happy thoughts of kissing Kyle and hearing him tell me he loved me.

Kyle continued reading, shaking his head back and forth slowly as he did.

My first impressions were quite favorable. She's a pleasant looking woman—not so attractive or unattractive as to be a distraction to either voters or her future husband. She has a pleasant demeanor and good fashion sense if we're to judge by the dress she wore last night.

But then things turned as south as our arrogant, flashy, pretentious Southern California neighbors. When I expressed my gratitude for wonderful people like those who run Mercy

House, Ms. Emerson expressed her disgust with the parents whose children are helped there, calling them selfish and abusive. When I expressed sorrow that many of these children have witnessed such sadness, she gloated over the fact that her family was affluent enough that her mother was there to greet her after school every day, and although she didn't go so far as to say it, I'd suspect she was wearing pearls and holding a plate of fresh-baked chocolate chip cookies.

When I reminded her the Aldsworth family has a son who has struggled with alcohol addiction, she lamented that every family has at least one black sheep, and when I asked her for something substantive about Kyle Aldsworth's character, her response was, 'He's handsome.'

While her tact and possibly her intelligence are certainly in question, one has to wonder if her judgmental and condescending outlook will serve Kyle Aldsworth well.

One thing's for certain. No matter how they dress her up, Charlotte Emerson is no Roberta Aldsworth.

Kyle folded up the newspaper, slowly at first and then faster and more forcefully, until he was finished. Then he flung it toward the fireplace and collapsed back into the couch. I was proud of myself. Even though I felt like crying, I'd kept the tears in check. And then Roberta sat down on the other side of me and gently laid her hand on my knee. It was like her hand had turned a faucet and the tears started flowing—big, hot, silent tears poured down my cheeks and dropped off my chin.

Kyle moved closer and folded his arms around me, pulling me into his chest. Now my tears soaked into his t-shirt.

"I don't want to be insensitive," Devon said after a

minute, "but we have to know what was said last night. We need to ask you some questions." Apparently, he'd been patient as long as he could. Now he needed answers.

Chapter 15

I pulled away from Kyle and patted the wet front of his shirt. "It's okay. You can ask me whatever you want. I didn't say those things."

"You never said the parents were selfish and abusive?" Donald asked.

I shook my head. "I said I felt sad for them, but Angela said they were selfish and abusive."

"And the thing about your family being so affluent that your mother was there to greet you after school every day?" Devon asked.

"My family isn't affluent. We're a normal family. And all I said was something like I was glad . . ." What exactly had I said? "I think I said I was glad I didn't have to worry about what I'd come home to."

"And what did you say about Alex being the black sheep?" Donald asked.

"I didn't say that. I said your family was great."

"Where did some of these things come from?" Donald was pacing.

Devon blew a breath through his nose and shook his head back and forth. He reminded me of a bull about to

158

charge. "It doesn't matter at this point who said what." My heart sank. Not only had I been misquoted, Angela had printed things I'd never say, and Devon didn't seem to believe me. Did Kyle? Did Donald and Roberta? "It's out there, and we've got to decide how we're going to combat it."

"What would you say our options are?" Roberta asked.

Devon paced in front of the fireplace. His head was slightly jutted forward, and his pointed nose and pursed lips made him look like an angry mouse. What was wrong with me? He was here to help fix something I'd done, and all I could do was compare him to the animal kingdom.

"Charlotte, would you step out into the hall for a minute?"

I looked at Kyle and then Roberta. Kyle squeezed my hand and then let go, so I got up and left, closing the door quietly behind me.

Suddenly, I felt angry. This was about me. This was something I'd supposedly done. And now I was waiting in the hall while they discussed how to handle me? The door was heavy, but I put my ear against it anyway.

"I guess I need to know if you're serious about this girl. Because our easiest way out of this mess would be to issue a statement saying you were no longer dating."

I tried to swallow but felt like I might choke. I listened hard to hear what Kyle would say, but it wasn't him who spoke next.

"She's a nice girl, Devon." It was Roberta.

"There are lots of nice girls." Devon said.

Then I heard Kyle's voice. Every muscle in my body strained, trying to help my ears make out his words. "I'm not going to . . . she didn't . . . other options." And then his voice got louder. "This is ridiculous. I'm not going to have her sitting in the hall like she's been sent to time out." His voice got louder, and I quickly stepped away from the door.

When the door opened, I was several feet away, looking at pictures on the wall, although I couldn't have told you anything specific about the photographs. If they were photographs. They might have been paintings.

"Hey." He stepped alongside me. I wanted to ask him what he'd said. Maybe some time I would.

"Kyle, I didn't say those things."

"I believe you."

"This is bad for you, isn't it?"

Kyle shrugged. "It's not good. But we can handle it. Devon's good, and Polly is on her way over."

"Who's Polly?"

"She's in public relations. Devon calls her in sometimes when things get . . . tricky."

I sighed. "Oh, Kyle. I'm so sorry."

Kyle shook his head and reached for my hand. "Let's go."

We'd barely sat back down on the couch together when the doorbell rang.

If Devon was a mouse, Polly was a bulldog. As soon as Roberta greeted her at the front door, Polly's voice carried throughout the house. "This is garbage. That woman should lose her job. What kind of yellow journalism is that? And why didn't someone prep this girl?" She rounded the corner into the office, her finger pointing at Devon. "Are you too busy, Devon? Or are you getting lazy?"

Devon straightened and met her accusing eyes. "Don't be coming in here telling me what we *should have* done. Let's figure out what needs done now."

"That sounds good, but if this girl"—she pointed at me— "is a long-term fixture in this family, someone should have prepped her. She was sitting at a table with media, for

160

crying out loud. What did you think? Angela Prescott would be content to talk about cupcakes and butterflies? The woman's had an agenda for years. You might as well have tossed her carcass into a cage of hyenas. I'm Polly, by the way." She put her hand out to shake mine.

Polly was tiny, not much more than five feet tall. I wasn't sure how her voice and her opinions could fit inside such a compact package.

"We're thinking we should have a press conference and have Charlotte make a statement," Devon said, and my heart landed somewhere on the thick rug at my feet.

Polly must have seen my expression. "You think that's a good idea?"

"Somehow, we have to get the word out there that Charlotte didn't say these things. She's assured us she didn't." I hated the way he said it, like there was a chance I was lying.

"Of course she didn't say it. Remember this is the same reporter"—Polly made giant air quotes—"who took that campaign worker to Vegas and tried to get the dirt on Donald." She turned toward Donald. "Thank you for keeping yourself out of the dirt." Donald nodded.

"Do you think you could make a statement?" Devon asked me.

Before I could answer, Polly held her hands up. "Now hold your horses. Let's not jump off a cliff to save a peanut butter sandwich." I had no idea what she was talking about, but somehow, Polly was making me feel a little better.

"That's why we called you, Polly. To keep us from jumping off a cliff," Donald said, and Devon huffed. "Sorry, Devon. We all know you're the best when it comes to political strategy, but when it comes to public relations messes"—I cringed—"we need Polly."

"I'm going to go have Allison fix some breakfast," Roberta said. "Why don't we leave Devon and Polly to strategize? Kyle, you take Charlotte home and let her get ready for the day. Let's all meet back here in an hour and a half, and we'll make a plan over breakfast."

"Sounds good to me," Polly said. "You woke me out of a dead sleep, and now that I'm awake, I'm starving."

Roberta pulled me into a quick hug before we left. "Don't worry. It'll all blow over."

The ride back to my apartment was quiet. I wanted to ask Kyle what he'd said when I'd been out of the room, but I didn't dare, and he didn't offer. Kyle circled my block twice, and when we still didn't find a parking place, he dropped me off and said he'd pick me back up in forty-five minutes. He squeezed my hand before I got out of the car.

My apartment was dark and quiet. I wished Mia was home to talk to. I needed to talk to someone. I thought about calling Mom and Dad, but knew I'd cause them worry. There was nothing they could do to fix this mess. They'd hear about it soon enough. I dialed McKayla's number.

"Hey, Sis," she said when she answered the phone. Before I could say anything, she continued, "We're out to breakfast with Connor's parents. Can I call you back later?"

"Sure."

She must have noticed the disappointment in my voice, because she instantly back-pedaled. "Unless there's something wrong? Are you okay?"

"Oh, sure. Later is fine." I made my voice as perky as possible.

"Okay. Good. You sounded upset for a second."

"No, I'm fine. Have fun. Give me a call later."

I dialed Angus's number before I'd even allowed myself to wonder if it was a good idea.

"Hey, Chuck, what's up?" His voice sounded so good, and that awful nickname so improper and unpolitical, that if he'd been in the same room with me, I'd have hugged him. I took a deep breath and let it out slowly. Somewhere in the exhalation, a sob escaped, and I covered my mouth with my hand. "Hey, is this Charlotte?"

"Yeah," I whispered around the lump in my throat.

"What's wrong?"

I shook my head, unable to speak. When he asked again, I realized he couldn't see me, and I'd have to give him something audible. "Have you seen the Chronicle this morning?"

"No. Why?"

"Do you have one there?"

"No, but I can pull it up online. What am I looking for?"

"Angela Prescott's article about the Mercy House benefit last night. Can you find it?"

"Yeah. Give me a second." I heard Angus's fingers tapping on the keyboard and voices in the background. "No, you guys go without me."

"I'm sorry, Angus. Did I interrupt plans?"

"We were headed out for a bike ride, but that's okay."

"No, you go ahead and go. We can talk later."

"Are you kidding? You're giving me a perfect excuse to bow out. I should be thanking you." I knew that wasn't true. Angus went bike riding whenever he could. It was his favorite way of dealing with the stress of medical school. "Okay, I'm there. Do you want me to read it aloud?"

"No. Just tell me when you're done."

I looked at the clock. I needed to be getting ready while he read. I put the phone on speaker and laid it on the bed while I changed into a pair of gray capris and a pale yellow lace top.

I was applying makeup when he finished. "Wow, Charles. What are you going to do?"

I leaned against the counter, feeling tired and weak. "I didn't say any of those things."

"Of course you didn't."

I sighed. "Thanks, Angus."

"I haven't done anything."

"Yes, you have. You knew I wouldn't say those horrible things."

"Have you talked to Kyle?"

I quickly recapped the dreadful morning. "He's picking me up in about fifteen minutes to go back and make a plan over breakfast. They're being nice about it, but I can tell everyone is pretty upset."

"Everyone including you."

"Yeah."

"I can imagine. But Charles, no one who knows you is going to believe a word of this."

"That's the problem, though. Most people who read this don't know me. They just think I'm being groomed to be the next Senator Aldsworth's wife. And they're probably deciding Kyle would be a terrible choice because of me."

"Are you two engaged?" Angus asked. There was a wariness in his tone.

"Of course not. I'd have told you if we were."

"Are you headed there?"

"I don't know. Kyle has said a few things that let me know he's looking down the road, and I'm in his plans. At least I was until this morning." Angus was quiet for long enough that I wondered if we'd been disconnected. "Are you there?" I asked.

"I'm here. Just thinking."

"What are you thinking?"

"I'm thinking if Kyle or his family let a nasty reporter change their minds about you, they're fools. And if they're that foolish, they're probably not fit for office."

I was ready to go, so I sat on the couch and watched for Kyle's car out the window. "Angus, I still don't know exactly how this happened. I was sitting there at the table, and she was being friendly and talkative, and I thought we were having polite dinner conversation. I'd never have imagined she'd come up with something like that article."

"It wasn't about you, Chuck. She obviously has an ax to grind with Senator Aldsworth."

"But why didn't I see it coming?"

"Because you judge other people by yourself. It's human nature. And you're not that way."

I saw Kyle's car round the corner. "Kyle's here. I've gotta go."

"Okay. Be strong. Don't let anyone bully you. Not nasty reporters and not the Senator's people. Remember, you're tough. You can handle anything."

"Thanks, Angus. Sorry you missed the bike ride."

"It's okay. I'm glad you called me."

Kyle leaned across the car and pushed the door open. Relief cooled my fevered worry when I saw his smile. "You look nice," Kyle said as he pulled into traffic.

I laughed. "You're always a gentleman. Even in a crisis. That's good to know."

Kyle turned to me after he pulled into a parking spot a couple of houses from his parents'. "I need to tell you something," he said, and I turned to face him. He rested his elbow on the back of my seat and fidgeted with my ponytail. "This isn't fatal. Devon and Polly are the best, and I'm sure they've figured out a way to make people forget this. Polly was right. We should have prepared you for this. We've been

165

doing this for so long, we forgot how new it is to you. You've never had to watch everything you say. You've probably never had any experience with people wanting to twist your words and use them against you. I'm sorry we didn't prepare you, but don't let this throw you. You'll learn the ropes. I'm sorry about this morning."

I didn't know how to explain my uneasiness. I knew Kyle was trying to comfort me, but I didn't feel comforted. I couldn't organize my thoughts into any rational order. But then Kyle's lips moved against mine, and I decided to sort things out later. The breathless ache his kiss caused was exactly what I needed to forget the horrible morning. I held him close and prolonged the kiss, not wanting to go back inside and face their "team."

I wanted to cry when Kyle pulled away, but I quickly gathered myself. I was glad to have Devon and Polly behind me, but even more grateful for Kyle and Angus.

Chapter 16

Over a breakfast of French toast, bacon, and orange juice, we discussed Angela Prescott's article and what we should do to combat it. According to Polly, it had been shared on Facebook forty-three times, tweeted over two hundred times, and the hashtag #dumpherkyle was trending in the bay area.

I wasn't sure what it meant for me and Kyle, but I knew it wasn't good.

"Maybe I should just disappear for a while." I was pleased my voice sounded strong.

"That doesn't work for me," Kyle said.

"We've got a plan," Polly said around a bite of food. She pointed her fork at Donald. "Call in a favor and get yourself on one of the Sunday morning shows, preferably *San Francisco Sunday Morning.* Tell them you want to discuss the jobs report that just came out. They'll be thrilled to have you, and you can be sure they'll ask something about Kyle and Charlotte. That will give you a chance to let everyone know you stand behind her."

Polly filled her mouth with another bite, so Devon took over. "You two are to be seen." He waved his hand back and forth between Kyle and me. "And I mean a lot. Everywhere. Mary Jameson is in charge at Mercy House on Sundays. You're to go tomorrow morning and take some of the kids to church services. We'll see that the papers hear about it. Go to dinner at a crowded restaurant every night for the next week. And I want you to look happy and be affectionate. Think Prince William and Kate. You're the new bay area royalty."

I thought I might throw up. It wasn't that I minded taking some of the kids from Mercy House to church or that it was a burden to eat out at nice places with Kyle every night. But they were choreographing my life. And I'm not a good dancer.

"We'll let you know where we want you to eat each night," Devon said to Kyle, and Kyle nodded. "We're taking charge of how you get spun, Charlotte, so you don't need to worry. We'll talk next weekend and see where we're at."

I tried to smile, but I don't think I succeeded. I was worried. Would I be able to pull off what they were asking of me? Kyle kissed my cheek and whispered in my ear. "See, it's all going to be fine."

I watched Donald on *San Francisco Sunday Morning* while I got ready for church. He looked distinguished in his gray suit and green, black and cream striped tie. He spoke eloquently of his plans to help turn the disappointing jobs report around. The show was nearly over. Maybe I wouldn't even get mentioned. That lifted my spirits a little. But then the host changed the subject.

"Before we let you go, Senator, we'd like to get your thoughts on one more matter. Over the weekend, an editorial in the Chronicle quoted your son's girlfriend, and it's created a lot of buzz. How are you and your family handling her unpopular, and frankly, disturbing, comments?"

"Well, Jim, I find it interesting that a real journalist would think the girl my son is dating is big news, but since she decided to make it an issue, I'll tell you this. I've come to know Charlotte, and I'm not buying what was in that editorial. If you look at Ms. Prescott's record, she has been prone to exaggeration and misquoting before, and unless she can back up her claims with proof of Charlotte's statements, I don't believe them. Charlotte is a lovely girl from a solid bay area family. She's talented and hard-working, and in all the time she's spent with Kyle and my family, we haven't seen a single indication she's anything other than a caring, thoughtful, and articulate woman."

"So you're saying Charlotte Emerson was misquoted?"

"I'm saying those quotes don't sound like the Charlotte we know and love."

"Are you making an announcement, Senator?"

Donald put up his hands. "Of course not. If there ends up being a wedding, I'd like to be invited." They laughed and Donald continued. "You watch. I think Charlotte is going to end up surprising and impressing a lot of people."

"Thanks for being on the show, Senator."

"Always a pleasure, Jim."

I appreciated what Donald had said, but I felt like this was someone else's life. How had I ended up being a topic of conversation on *San Francisco Sunday Morning*? It didn't feel like they could possibly be talking about me.

Kyle and I rang the doorbell at Mercy House, and Mary Jameson came to the door. "Thank you for coming. There will be three children going to church with you. Two are siblings, Cade and Abigail. Their mother is in rehab, and there's no father in the picture. The third child is a little older. Her name is Kyra. Her father died in Iraq, and her mother is also in court-ordered rehab as a condition of avoiding prison time."

"Can we take them to lunch after services?" Kyle asked.

"Of course. We'll just have you sign into the register and record the time you plan to have them back."

The children were charming. Cade and Abigail were six and eight and talked constantly. Kyra was eleven and shy. She responded softly when we spoke to her, but never initiated a conversation.

When church was over, Kyle took a vote, and all three kids wanted to eat at In-N-Out.

"What would you like?" Kyle asked them when we reached the cash register.

"Can we each have a hamburger?" Cade asked.

"Of course."

"Can we split some French fries?" Abigail asked.

"You can each have your own."

"Really?"

"You sure can." Kyle said. Cade punched the air, and Abigail grinned so wide her eyes almost disappeared.

"What would you like, Kyra," I asked.

"A milkshake, if that's okay."

"What else?"

"That's enough," she said.

"Aren't you hungry?"

She shrugged.

"I'm starving," I said. "I'll bet you're hungry too, aren't you?"

"A little. But I can wait 'til we get back to Mercy House."

"You don't have to wait. You can have a milkshake and a hamburger."

"And fries, too," Kyle said and ordered the works for everyone.

I was sad when it was time to leave the children at Mercy House. It had been a lovely few hours, and I'd been surprised and touched by how sweet and grateful the children had been. They thanked us, and we gave hugs all around. Abigail came back for a second hug before they waved goodbye and went inside.

I felt like a shirt that had been sitting in the bottom of the hamper for a month. Even though Devon and Polly had said we were to eat out at a nice restaurant every night for a week, I asked Kyle if we could count In-N-Out and call it a day.

"You're exhausted, aren't you?"

I nodded against the back of my seat as I watched him. "I think I need a nap and some time to regroup."

"You want me to come up with you?" The thought was tempting, but I knew if I wanted to sort through the weekend's events and gear myself up for the next week, it wasn't a good idea.

"You know if you come up, we'll end up doing more kissing than napping, so I think you'd better go and get those lips as far from me as possible." Kyle laughed and shook his head. "What?" I asked.

"Sometimes you surprise me." He pulled into the closest open spot at the curb, almost a block from my apartment. "Do you want me to walk back with you?"

"That's okay. You're in a loading zone."

Kyle put the car in park and turned toward me. "Am I allowed to kiss you goodbye, or will that be too tempting?"

I put my hand on his cheek and kissed him—a couple of

short kisses and then a longer one. "See?" I rested my forehead against his. "This is why you can't come up."

"I understand." He kissed the tip of my nose. "I'll talk to you tomorrow."

I fully intended to nap the rest of the day, but my friends and family rightfully thought Sunday afternoon would be a good time to call and offer their love and support, and although the day didn't include much sleeping, I felt better with every phone call.

Dad and Mom called just after I'd stretched out on my bed. They sympathized with me about the Angela Prescott disaster. They were happy to hear I had the Aldworths and their people behind me.

"Imagine being ordered to eat out at nice restaurants every night," Dad said.

"Try to enjoy yourself through all this, Charlotte. Remember, you're not just doing PR for Kyle's campaign. He's also courting you, so be sure that doesn't get lost in the shuffle." It was no wonder I loved my parents. Dad was looking at the positive angle, and Mom was looking out for my feelings. And she'd used the word "courting." Such a cute, vintage word.

Roberta called, mostly to be my cheerleader. "You're doing great."

"Tell her she's being a trooper," I heard Donald say in the background.

"Did you hear that, Charlotte? Don says you're being a trooper."

Will and Gina called together. "That article was terrible," Gina said.

"Sorry you're not beautiful enough to be more of a distraction," Will said.

"Not funny, Will." Gina hated it when Will teased me.

"Actually, it's kinda funny," I said. "Did you know at dinner that night, she called me stunning? Which one is the lie? The one she said in person or the one she printed?"

"You've always been beautiful," Gina said.

"Will, when are you going to convince your wife that I love her even without the flattering words?"

"Sorry, Chuckers. They're only flattering words if they're not sincere. She tells me you're beautiful even when you're not around, so I'm pretty sure she means it."

"You guys are just trying to boost my confidence for all this media nonsense."

"Is it working?" Will asked.

"Well, it's not hurting, I guess. But Will, seriously, you've got to stop calling me Chuck and Chuckers. The media will take those and run with them. And then I'll have to hurt you."

"She's right, Will. You've got to stop."

"You have a point," he admitted. "I'll do my best to limit the nicknames to the privacy of our homes."

"How about you do your best to eliminate them entirely?" I didn't even want to think about #Chuck or #Chuckers trending.

McKayla was sick that she hadn't stepped outside and talked to me on Saturday morning when I'd called her. I assured her it was fine, but she felt guilty for letting me down in my hour of need. "By the way, if it goes according to their plan, people are going to be paying attention to you. No more wearing Will's basketball warmups."

"I can still wear them around the house." I picked a string off the sweatpants that said "slammin'" down the leg. No way was I admitting I had them on right now.

"You should get rid of them."

"Let's stop talking about what I'm wearing and talk

173

about Dad's birthday."

"You're wearing them?"

"I didn't say that."

"Yes, you did. You're hopeless. And Dad's birthday isn't for two months."

"I know. But we should throw him a good party this year. You don't turn forty-eight every year."

"You don't turn any age every year."

I sighed. "I know that. I just want to talk about something other than me, or Kyle and me, or media junk. I'm kinda sick of it."

"All right. Well then, let's plan Dad's birthday party." Thank you, McKayla.

Angus called Sunday evening to see how I was doing. I hadn't napped at all, but I was feeling better after the rah rah phone calls from my family and a grilled cheese sandwich I'd eaten for dinner. When Angus knew I was fine, he handed the phone to Wyatt.

"Charlotte, I'm so sorry. If I'd had any idea what she was going to pull, I'd have put her across the table from you. Or on the other side of Kyle. I felt sick when I heard what she'd done."

"It wasn't your fault. Don't feel bad."

"But I do. There were actually some nice people at that table."

"She seemed pretty nice while we were eating dinner."

"Well, I feel awful. I wanted you to know I'm sorry."

"Don't worry. It's fine. And the night was a huge success, so you should be celebrating, not worrying about me."

"It was a good night for Mercy House, that's for sure. And it was a pretty good night for my career, too, I think. Some pretty influential people have my name now. That's

174

partly thanks to you introducing me to the Aldsworths, so thank you. Oh, there's the timer. We've got cookies in the oven. Anyway, sorry about that woman." She said "that woman" like it was a curse word.

"No fair," I said when Angus got back on the phone. "I want cookies. Did you make your chocolate chip cookies?"

"Is there any other kind?"

"Are they loaded with walnuts?"

"Wyatt isn't a big nut fan, so we only did half with walnuts."

"Eat a few for me."

The phone rang right after I hung up.

"Are you bringing me some cookies?" I said instead of hello.

"Uh, is that what you want?" It was Aleena. I laughed.

"Sorry. Angus and his girlfriend made chocolate chip cookies, and I was hoping he was offering to run a plate over."

"I thought maybe you wanted some fortune cookies. You know, hoping for a little good luck?"

I sighed. "Oh man, I could certainly use some good luck."

"Do you want me to make up a fortune for you?"

"How about one that says, 'Your future is terrifying. Eat more chocolate chip cookies.'"

"Not very Chinese. How about 'Your future is full of big changes' or 'the world will soon know your name.'"

I lay back on the couch and propped my feet up on the back. "Aleena, it probably sounds exciting, but this weekend was hard. I'm not sure I'm cut out for all this."

"You need to change your attitude. This is an adventure. You've got a handsome man who obviously likes you a lot. If you marry him, you'll probably never have another financial worry. You'll get to travel and see places. You'll have a successful husband. If you think about it, it doesn't sound too bad."

"You're right. I need an attitude adjustment. I'm sure the good outweighs the bad. And Kyle is amazing."

"Exactly. Keep that in mind, and you can deal with the rest of it. And if you don't want him, send him my way. I'm not opposed to a Charlotte castoff. Especially if he looks like Kyle."

Aleena was exactly right. I could get through this. I just needed to have the right attitude. I needed to concentrate on the pros instead of the cons. Maybe I should make myself a list to remind me. After I got ready for bed, I got out a notebook and sat on the floor against the bed, making myself a visual. Of course, it needed to be colorful and eye-catching, so I pulled out my colored pens and got to work.

I wrote "pros" in orange—because it's my favorite color—on one side of the paper and "cons" in brown on the other side. I didn't dislike the color brown. I actually didn't dislike any color, but brown looked the least exciting at the moment.

Under "pros," I made my list: Kyle, financial security, nice family, traveling, great clothes, Kyle, eating at great restaurants, probably someone who'd clean my bathrooms, cute little Kyles running around, KYLE'S KISSES (that deserved to be capitalized), a nice house, Kyle, Kyle, Kyle.
I moved to the "cons" list, but before I started writing, I looked at all the good things I'd put on the left side of the paper. Sure, there would be cons, but I didn't want to dwell on them. I didn't even want to think about them. I was going to accentuate the positive. I put a big X through the cons side. Then I taped the list to the wall by my bed so I could see it every morning before I got out of bed.

Chapter 17

"You're making quite a splash," Jayne said when she came into my office.

"Oh, Jayne. You wouldn't even believe the weekend I had."

"Actually, I probably would. You've been all over the place. Television, papers, internet."

I buried my head in my hands. "This is so out of my comfort zone."

"You're doing fine. The pictures of you with the kids were cute."

"What are you talking about?"

"The pictures of you with the kids. Coming out of the church and at In-N-Out."

I groaned.

"Go to the Chronicle. You'll see them."

Sure enough, there we were with the children. The pictures were cute. Cade and Abigail were laughing, and Kyra was holding my hand as we left the church. At the restaurant, the camera was behind the children, but Kyle and I were looking at each other and smiling, although I was shoving a French fry in my mouth at the same time. "Of course I'm eating."

"Oh, stop it. You look cute."

"I didn't even know there was a photographer. How can I be so oblivious to everything? And what about the kids? I'm not sure they should have taken pictures of the kids."

"You worry too much," Jayne said.

"If you'd had the weekend I just had, you'd be worrying, too."

"Stop worrying and enjoy the ride. Kyle likes you. I'd bet money you're engaged by the end of the summer."

"That's only six weeks away."

Jayne shrugged. "Like I said. The end of the summer. Want to wager?"

"No. Someone will find out and splash it all over the internet."

"See, you're catching on to this just fine."

Mia: hey, girl. we need 2 catch up 2night. i'm craving curry. i'm picking up ingredients. chicken or shrimp?

Mia: graham will be there. you should invite ur man.

I hadn't seen Mia since Saturday morning. It would be nice to spend the evening in the apartment, stuffing ourselves on curry. Unfortunately, that wasn't our assignment.

Me: Oh man, I wish we could. We need to talk. But I have to go out tonight.

Mia: you'd rather go out than have my curry?

Me: No way. I'd rather have your curry any day. It's a long story. Like I said, we need to talk.

Mia: ru going out with kyle?

Me: Yes.

Mia: whew! you had me scared for a minute.

Me: Sorry. Can we talk when I get home?

Mia: it's a date.

I was planning to work right through lunch so I could leave a little early, but then Angus walked in with a Ziplock bag full of cookies, and I changed my plans.

"Still want some cookies?"

"I always want cookies." I opened the bag. "Oh good, these have walnuts."

"I know better than to bring nutless cookies to you."

I opened the bag and took a bite. "These don't taste like day-old cookies."

"I kept out some of the dough and baked them this morning."

"For me?"

"And me." Angus reached for a cookie and took a bite.

"Thanks, Angus. These are perfection." Angus sat in a chair across the desk from me and stretched out his long legs. He bit on the side of his mouth, a habit that told me he was apprehensive. "Is everything okay?"

"I come bearing more than cookies. I have news."

I leaned forward in my chair. "Spill it."

"Well, I've made a decision. About my residency. I'm headed to New York."

"Oh." He might as well have hit me in the chest with a bowling ball. Of course, I'd known New York was one of his options, but I'd never envisioned him actually leaving. Not with Alameda so close and also an option. There were so many reasons to stay. "Wow. That's great," I tried to sound like I meant it. "What made you choose New York?"

"A few things. It'd be nice to see another part of the world. I don't have anything tying me down yet. And . . . I don't know." Something wasn't quite right. There was something he wasn't telling me.

"What about Wyatt?"

"What about her?"

"I thought you two were getting along."

"She's great. But I don't love her."

"Maybe you could. If you stayed, I mean."

Angus sighed and sat up in his seat. "Wyatt and I are good friends. We like to hang out together. But that's all."

"I can tell she likes you. Maybe—"

"Don't Chuck. Let's please not analyze me and Wyatt."

"Okay. I'm sorry." I'd obviously touched a nerve. "I guess I just wanted you to take the Alameda position."

"Why?"

"Because New York's a long ways away, and I'll miss you."

Angus leaned forward, his elbows on his knees. He shook his head. "Charlotte?" He was upset. He hadn't called me Charlotte since high school.

He'd been helping me with calculus. He'd gone through an entire problem, trying to explain how to do it. When he'd gotten the answer, he looked up and found me writing the word "calculus" in a flowery script. "What are you doing, Charlotte?" he'd said.

"Sorry, I don't get calculus," I'd said.

"And you never will if you don't try." He'd closed his book and walked to the door. "Let me know when you actually care enough to try."

The next day I'd apologized for my lack of focus, and he'd helped me study. Desperate to show him I was truly sorry, I'd concentrated on everything he'd shown me. I got an A on that test—my first calculus A of the year.

But why was he upset now? What had I done? "Is something wrong?" I asked. Angus dropped back in his chair and ran his hand over his face. "Have I done something wrong?" When he didn't immediately answer, I wondered if he'd heard me.

"No, you haven't done anything wrong. I'll miss you too. I'll miss you and Will and, well, all of you. But it's time for me to try something new."

"Are you excited?" He'd worked so hard. I wanted him to be happy about what he was doing next, but right now, he just seemed angry. Angry and frustrated and . . . sad.

"Sure. New York looks great."

"Maybe we can come visit you."

"Yeah. That'd be fun."

"I'm sorry I've been such a horrible friend. I was so caught up in everything that happened this weekend, I didn't even ask you about your residency."

"That's okay. You had a lot on your mind."

"That's not an excuse for being a bad friend. You've had a lot on your mind, too, and you checked on me last night."

Angus shrugged. "I'd better go." He looked tired as he pulled himself out of the chair. I hurried over to his side of the desk.

"Want another cookie?"

"Nah. Those were for you."

181

"Thanks. They're delicious." I suddenly felt the urge to hug Angus. I put my arms around his waist and hugged him close. At first he didn't respond, and I felt silly and awkward. Then his arms came around me, and his body relaxed into mine.

This was unusual. We never spontaneously hugged each other. Sure, there were the little hugs at family birthdays, but the only times we hugged each other were when we were going for therapy. Ah, therapy. "Are you and Wyatt still dating?"

"Yeah. We still hang out."

"So you're not in need of any therapy?"

I felt Angus's breath in my hair when he laughed. "I probably always need therapy. But that kind of therapy? Not yet."

"Well, let me know," I said. I felt a little sad for Angus and Wyatt. They seemed like a perfect match.

That night we ate at The Platinum Spoon. Kyle was a little distracted, but when I asked him if something was wrong, he shook his head and stayed attentive the rest of the evening. At least until the ride home. He'd barely said a word since we'd left the restaurant.

"Are you sure nothing's wrong? You look worried."

"I'm not worried, just frustrated."

"About what?" I turned in my seat to face him.

"Devon called. They've arranged for us to accidentally meet Frank Stapley and his fiancé tomorrow night at dinner."

"Accidentally?"

"Yeah. This is the part of politics I hate."

"Who's Frank Stapley?"

Kyle laughed. "I guess it's a good thing we're talking about this."

"Should I know him?"

"According to me, no. According to Devon and Polly, you probably should. He's kinda high society San Francisco. Lots of money. Always on the society pages. Until he got engaged, we were both on the 'most eligible bachelor' list."

Now it was my turn to laugh. "There's a list?"

"It was in *San Francisco Today* magazine."

"Who was ranked higher?" I asked, playing with the hair on the back of his neck.

"Who do you think?" Kyle tried to sound indignant, but his smile gave him away.

"You, of course."

"Of course."

"Ooh, am I a lucky girl or what?"

"Anyway, we're supposed to run into Frank and his fiancé and then end up eating dinner together. I'm sure it will end up in some paper or magazine."

"What does one wear to have dinner with not one, but two of San Francisco's most eligible bachelors?"

"You always look great. I'm not worried. I just hate all this planning and orchestrating. It feels fake."

"That's because it is fake."

Kyle looked surprised.

"I don't mean you're fake," I quickly said. "I mean this meeting is fake."

Kyle didn't respond, and we rode in silence for a few minutes.

"Are you worried about this because of me?"

Kyle still didn't respond.

"Kyle? Are you worried about me?"

He sighed. "I'm always worried about you."

"You think I'm going to blow it? Say something stupid?"

"No, Charlotte. I don't think you're going to blow it. It's just that this is all new to you, and I didn't want you to have to deal with it yet. I wanted to be able to break you in and have you get used to this crazy life slowly. I don't want you to feel all this pressure."

Now it was my turn to think. He said he wasn't worried about me blowing it, but I already had. Sort of. I hadn't been careful enough, and I'd given a political enemy enough to write an unflattering article. How could he not be a little afraid I'd do something wrong and embarrass him and his family?

"I'll be careful," I said. "I'll watch what I say."

Kyle gave me a half smile. "I'm sorry for all of this. I'm sorry I want to take Dad's spot. I'm sorry the media is awful. And I'm sorry you're getting thrown into it all without a safety net." Kyle parked the car.

Something was troubling me, but changing it from a fleeting thought, almost a feeling, into words was difficult. It wasn't until I was washing my face that it came to me. I didn't want to do any of this without a safety net. If we were going to move forward, shouldn't we be the safety net for each other? If we were falling for each other, didn't we need to be there to catch each other? No matter what happened?

Chapter 18

We ate at Posh, a French and Asian fusion restaurant that was all about pretense. I'd never been inside a place that tried so hard to make such a literal statement. Gold-leafed French provincial furniture mixed with Asian silkscreened art in black lacquered frames seemed at odds with each other. I hoped the food fused the two styles better than the décor.

A harp played slightly dissonant music in the background. Sconces with gold veining lined the walls.

"Kyle? Is that you?"

Great. Was this Frank?

"Frank?" Kyle said. Yep, it was Frank.

"I thought that was you." Frank was nearly shouting. Most of the faces that lined the entryway benches waiting for tables were now trained on us. I towered several inches over Frank, but he definitely had me on bulk. His gray fitted shirt stretched over his wide shoulders and redwood-sized biceps. His neck was wider than his head. These looked like enhanced gym muscles, not the kind that come from athletics. Even his fingers looked beefy. His gelled hair was slicked back, mafia style. He either traveled regularly to tropical locations or frequented the Tan-Fastic salon because he was a shade that doesn't come naturally in San Francisco's often rainy climate.

"How ya doin, man?" Frank bellowed. "I haven't seen you since, when? Was it that bachelor's charity auction three years ago?"

"That was it. It's good to see you. This is Charlotte." Kyle's hand at my back guided me to the center of the conversation.

"Charlotte, it's a pleasure," Frank said. He didn't give any indication that he was bothered by having to look up at me. I gave him a point for that. He pumped my arm with gusto. "And this is Tiffany." He put his arms out to a woman who came from farther inside the restaurant. With her five inch heels, she was almost as tall as me, which made her taller than Frank. I grudgingly gave him another point. The sequins on her short, purple dress flashed in the light. I've never had a desire to wear a dress of solid sequins, but they certainly made my red flowered dress look plain in comparison.

"Sorry, I was in the ladies room," Tiffany said.

"Tiffany, this is Kyle and Charlotte. Kyle's also an eligible bachelor." He lowered his voice. "He was two spots ahead of me on the list, but what do they know, right?" He laughed.

"It looks like you've been on that list for the last time," Kyle said.

"I finally found someone worth getting off the list for." Frank nudged Tiffany. "Show them your ring."

Tiffany held out her hand. I was surprised she had the strength to hold up her arm. The pink diamond in the center had to be four carats, and that wasn't even counting the row of diamonds surrounding it.

"Wow. That's beautiful," I said. "Congratulations."

"You sure you know what you're getting into with this guy?" Kyle asked. Was it my imagination, or was he talking a little louder than usual?

"I'm sure." Tiffany snuggled down into Frank's shoulder.

"You should join us for dinner," Kyle said.

"Why not?" said Frank.

"I'll see if they can adjust our reservation."

Kyle stepped over to the hostess stand, and she quickly nodded. When she didn't make any changes to her list, it occurred to me the reservation might have already been made for four.

"Can they seat us together?" Frank asked.

"She said it wasn't a problem," Kyle said.

It was only a few minutes until the hostess called our names and took us to a table in the middle of the restaurant. I looked around the room at the quiet tables set against the walls and felt jealous of the people sitting in all those less conspicuous places.

Frank and Tiffany were friendly, pleasant, and loud, which is probably what Devon had hoped for. We definitely demanded attention. The men talked sports and politics while Tiffany talked about wedding plans and movies she'd seen recently. I was happy to let her take the lead. I didn't want to say the wrong thing.

"I just had my hair colored by Jean Paul over at Zissors." Tiffany ran her fingers through her dark hair. "We're doing a trial run for the wedding. To see if we like it, and if it looks good with the bridesmaid dresses and flowers."

"It looks pretty. I like the color," I said.

"You should totally go to him. He could give your hair

some nice highlights and shine. It'd give your face a great lift."

"Maybe I will," I said, though I had no intention of going to anyone but McKayla.

"If you go, be sure to tell Jean Paul I sent you. Don't forget, he's at Zissors. With a Z."

I nodded.

"I adore him. He actually helped me make a final decision on my wedding dress. He has an eye for style. I told him he should do hair part-time and become a personal stylist. Every time I go to him, he makes great suggestions on ways to pump up an outfit. He knows how to add a little sizzle." Tiffany shimmied a little, and Frank watched her appreciatively.

"So Jean Paul's the one I need to thank for the sizzle, huh?" he asked.

Tiffany kissed Frank on the cheek. "See, Frankie, I told you Jean Paul is worth every penny." They kissed loudly.

Kyle slid his seat a little toward the corner so he'd be closer and rested his arm on the back of my chair. I was glad I was here with him.

"You two make an adorable couple," Tiffany said.

"Kyle's always had good taste in women," Frank said. "When we did that bachelor auction, the woman I wanted to win me didn't even bid. She was saving all her money for that guy." He pointed at Kyle with both hands. "And she got him. Why didn't anything happen with her? She was a tasty little number."

There was nothing to say to this, and even Kyle, who was usually unflappable, shifted in his seat.

"We went to dinner. Like the auction required."

"Nothing else? I could have sworn the sparks were flying that night. I thought she might be a keeper."

Kyle looked calm and cool, except for his ears that had turned bright red. "So how did you two meet?" Kyle asked Tiffany.

"We met at a club." Tiffany giggled. "We're just one, big cliché."

"A happy cliché," Frank said.

I was disappointed when the food arrived. I was hungry, and the plating was more about looking artistic than satiating an appetite. Giant square plates showcased a drizzle of some buttery, French sauce with a single eggroll. When those plates were removed, and the entrée arrived, it was on an oval plate the size of a small sofa. In the center of the plate was a little mound of noodles with a creamy sauce and three strips of braised beef.

"Can we interest you in some dessert?" the waiter asked.

"Not if I hope to fit in my wedding dress," Tiffany said. I found that amusing. If the desserts were proportionate to the rest of the meal, she'd have trouble even tasting it.

"I'm too smart to eat dessert in front of her." Frank shook his head.

And with that, any hopes I had of leaving the restaurant satisfied vanished. Kyle and Frank squabbled about who would pay for dinner. Kyle finally prevailed, and soon we were making our way through the restaurant for the front doors. Several diners stopped eating or talking to watch us walk by. One man stopped Frank long enough to shake hands and ask about a body-building event he was planning to enter. It became clear they knew each other from the gym. Since Kyle and I were behind Frank and Tiffany, we were forced to stand awkwardly between two tables while they talked. I did my best not to make eye contact or look at what the people around us were eating.

As Frank made protein supplement recommendations,

a wave of uneasiness crashed over me. I felt trapped and needed air. I tried to inhale, but my lungs went on lockdown about halfway into the breath and I couldn't get enough oxygen. I took a few shallow breaths and tried again with no luck.

"That's Senator Aldsworth's son and his girlfriend," someone whispered.

"Do you think he'll run?" someone else said.

I didn't hear the answer. My pulse was pounding in my ears and behind my eyes. It thrummed louder and louder until I no longer knew if Frank was talking about body building or gold mining. The room became a tilt-o-whirl. I tried to focus on Tiffany's sequined dress, but the sparkles were spinning with the room. Kyle was behind me. I knew because I could feel his hand on my waist.

Finally, Frank stopped talking and started walking. I took a couple of tentative steps, but I was like a child who'd been twirling on the lawn. It felt like I was at a forty-five degree angle to the floor. My balance had abandoned me, and I reached for the closest table to hold myself up just as my legs buckled.

"Charlotte?" Kyle said as one of my hands missed the table and instead knocked over a glass of water.

"I'm so sorry" I held tightly to the edge of the table. "I'm so dizzy."

"Is she drunk?" someone asked.

"I'm sorry," Kyle said to someone. "Here Charlotte." I felt his arm tighten around me, and I managed to stand straight. The room was still swirling, so I put my arm around Kyle and leaned into him. He guided me through the rest of the tables and toward the door.

"Is something wrong?" It was the hostess who had hurried to meet us.

I put my hand up to my head. "I need some air."

"I'll take her outside," Kyle said. "I think she's fine."

On the sidewalk, Kyle guided me to the wide windowsill of a closed hearing aid store, and I leaned my head against the wall, trying to get a breath. Tiffany and Frank stood in front of me. Kyle was beside me, holding my hand.

After a few minutes, Frank and Tiffany stopped dancing in front of my eyes, and I was able to fill my lungs with air. "I'm so sorry. I don't know what happened. I was so dizzy, and I felt like I was going pass out."

"It's okay. Are you feeling better now?" Kyle had moved beside me and smoothed my head against his side.

"I'll be fine." I tried to stand, but I felt a little shaky and held tightly to Kyle's hand.

After an awkward goodbye to Frank and Tiffany, we walked slowly to Kyle's car.

I didn't know what to say. What had been a dizzy spell in the restaurant now settled into a dread I couldn't speak aloud. Kyle was quiet, too, and I wondered if he was feeling the cloud of fear I felt. I'd just made a scene.

I leaned my head against the seat and closed my eyes, but when all I could see behind my eyelids was the restaurant spinning like a top, I opened them and anchored them on the dashboard in front of me.

"What happened in there?" Kyle asked.

"I'm not sure. At first I just felt trapped and claustrophobic, but then I got so dizzy I couldn't stand up straight."

"Are you okay now?"

"I'm still a little dizzy," I admitted. "But it's getting better.

Kyle nodded. I wanted to ask him what he was thinking, but I didn't dare.

Kyle walked me up to my apartment and unlocked the
door for me. Mia and Graham were sitting on the couch
watching television when we walked into the room. When
Mia saw me leaning on Kyle, she hurried over to meet us.

"I'm glad you're home," Kyle said. "I didn't want to
leave her here alone."

"What happened?"

"I'm fine." I wanted to go to bed.

"She had a dizzy spell at the restaurant. Nearly went
down."

Kyle led me to my room, Mia close behind him. "I'm
going to lie down for a few minutes before I get ready for
bed." I pulled a blanket over me, and Kyle pulled it up to my
chin while Mia tucked it around my feet.

I reached for Kyle's hand, and he sat down on the edge
of the bed. Mia slipped out of the room, pulling the door
closed behind her.

"I'm sorry," I said. Kyle held my hand in both of his. He
didn't answer, just sat there looking at my hand between his.
"I don't think I've ever apologized as much as I have lately."
Kyle still didn't respond. He seemed deep in thought. "Please
don't be angry at me," I whispered.

"I'm not angry." I wanted him to look at me—not at my
hand. At me. But he didn't for a long time. Finally, he turned
to me. "Are you okay? If I go, I mean."

I was glad he was now looking at me, because I was
afraid if I tried to speak, I might start to cry. I nodded.

Kyle leaned over and kissed my forehead. "I'll talk to
you tomorrow. Get some rest." I nodded again.

He turned off the light and closed the door as he left. I
could hear his voice outside my room. He was talking to Mia.
And then he was gone, and Mia was peeking through the
door.

"Do you need anything?"

"No. I'm good," I said, even as tears soaked my pillow.

"Call me if you do." She closed the door softly.

I rolled over and faced the wall. I couldn't bear the thought of what Devon and Polly would think of tonight or the worry I'd cause Donald and Roberta. I ached when I thought of Kyle and how he must feel. Did he regret ever letting Jayne set us up? Did he still love me, or did he wish he'd never said those words? I had to do better. I couldn't have panic attacks—or whatever that had been tonight—if I was to be a good wife for Kyle. I needed to carry myself with grace and dignity, and I needed to control my emotions. I'd have to watch my words and keep them above reproach. I'd need to dress appropriately, just like Roberta had explained. McKayla was right. Tomorrow, I was throwing away the "slammin'" sweatpants. And a whole lot more. I'd take a whole garbage bag full of clothes to the Goodwill—everything that was too casual, too flashy, or too immature. Goodbye, Tweety t-shirt.

I could do this. I would make Kyle and his parents proud. I'd become a political asset instead of a liability. Starting tomorrow, I'd become a new Charlotte. Maybe I'd even go see Jean Paul, and he could help me with both my hair and my overall style.

I finally fell asleep hugging my new resolve close.

Chapter 19

Thankfully, the rest of the week went according to plan. I skipped lunch the next day and had time between work and dinner to purge my closet of all clothing that might embarrass a senator. Anything a little too ragged, short, or outdated went in the bag. I put the bag by the front door so I could drop it off on my way to work the next morning. Then I dressed for dinner.

Kyle had texted me with the dinner plans, and my stomach had been celebrating ever since. It was a popular place called The Farmhouse and it was famous for the generous plates of organically grown meats and vegetables. It sounded delicious, and it was. I ate baked chicken, roasted vegetables, and even had a slice of strawberry rhubarb pie with vanilla ice cream.

We didn't "run into" anyone for dinner, and Kyle was relaxed and happy. It felt like a date we'd have had three weeks ago. I put his political plans out of my mind and enjoyed being with him.

On Saturday morning, we met with Devon and Polly at the Aldsworths' house. It was a mostly positive meeting. Of course, they weren't thrilled that I'd had a near-death experience at Posh (okay, that was an exaggeration), but it hadn't been too devastating. I hadn't even known what had happened because of my "spell," and I was surprised it had been both discussed and handled.

"Someone who had dinner at Posh called into *The Kat and Teegan Show*." I must have looked confused because Polly explained. "Kat and Teegan have a morning talk show on AM radio. Anyway, someone called in and wanted to know if Kyle Aldsworth's girlfriend was a lush."

I gasped. "I don't even drink."

"We know," Devon said. "Don't worry. I had Tammy from my office call in a few minutes later. She made an unofficial statement for the Aldsworth family, letting listeners know you don't drink, and you've been putting in long hours at work, as well as helping your sister-in-law through her pregnancy, and making public appearances with Kyle. Once she hung up, Kat and Teegan had a whole conversation about how hard it is to keep up with everything, and how much more difficult it is when you're in the public eye. Teegan mentioned the stress of celebrities like Lindsay Lohan and Miley Cyrus, who have had public breakdowns because they're so worn out, and how embarrassing that must be for them to have the public watching them during their difficult times. They encouraged everyone to give you the benefit of the doubt."

"So that little dizzy spell actually worked to our advantage," Polly said.

"But don't think we want it to happen again." Devon was such a warm fellow.

At first, I was disturbed because they already knew I didn't drink. And then I wondered how they knew I'd been helping Gina. Worst of all, though, was being compared to Lindsay or Miley. I was glad they were happy about an averted crisis, but I was starting to feel like my life had become the victim of a hostile takeover.

"I think you two can go about living your lives for now." Polly was smiling like we'd all scored a major victory. "Of course, be aware of what's going on, watch what you say, and use good judgment, but for the time being, I think you're in good shape.

Kyle practically floated out of the house. His step was light, and he kissed me before we got in the car. I didn't want to spoil his good mood by asking how they knew about Gina, so I let it slide.

It was nice being back to normal. I still saw Kyle almost every day, but instead of worrying about being seen, we did what we wanted. We went to a movie. We made brownies at my apartment. We even ate fast food one night when Kyle was craving a bacon cheeseburger. I tried to look nice and put together whenever I left the apartment, and I was careful not to talk to strangers, but mostly, I didn't worry too much.

I'd just snuggled under my covers when I heard the apartment door slam. Then I heard Mia crying. I got out of bed and opened the door. "What's going on?"

"Nothing," Mia said between sobs.

I ignored her and put my arms around her. She cried into my shoulder for a couple of minutes and then pulled away and headed to the box of Kleenexes on the coffee table. I sat in the corner of the couch and pulled my legs up under me. "Do you feel like talking?"

"Not really." She blew her nose. "I'm so stupid."

"No you're not."

"I am, too. I don't know why I can't just be patient."

"Because some of us struggle with patience," I said. "It's not our fault. It's our nature to be impatient."

"Oh, Charlie, I did a dumb thing tonight. I pushed him again."

"Pushed him how?" We hadn't turned the light on, and I wasn't about to now. Mia seemed to feel more comfortable spilling her heart out to me in the dark.

"We were having such a nice time. We'd been talking about some problems he's been having with some employees at work, and I was giving him some suggestions. He said he was glad he could talk to me about things. It made it easier to know what to do. And then I said we make a good team, and he said he was glad I was on his side. And then I said I knew a way he could be sure I'd always be on his side. Why did I say that?"

"Is there something wrong with saying that?" I asked.

"There must be, because he said, Mia, don't start on me. Please. And I said, I'm not starting anything. Just pointing out the obvious. I thought I was being funny, but he got all serious and said you're not going to start nagging again, are you?" I tried not to laugh at Mia's impersonation of Graham's voice. "I told him I wasn't nagging. He said things were going great between us, and he thinks when he does feel ready to get married, he'll want me to be the one, but he isn't interested in listening to me whine about when he'll be ready. So I told him he didn't need to listen to me whine or do anything else ever again, if he didn't want to. So he brought me home and that's that."

Mia started sniffling again. "It doesn't sound fatal. I'll bet he calls you tomorrow, and things will be fine.

"No, he won't." I could see Mia's head shaking in the dark. "He said maybe he'll call when he's ready to get married and maybe he won't. What if I've blown it this time?"

"If you can't even have this conversation, I'm not sure why you want him. Why is he so sensitive?"

"I'm sure it's his parents. His mom has been married three times, and his dad's been married five."

"Whoa. I didn't know that. I guess that explains a lot."

"Which is why I shouldn't be so stupid."

I walked over to the chair where Mia was sitting, pulled her up, and hugged her again. "You're not stupid. He missed you last time. I'm sure he'll miss you again. Get some sleep. You'll feel better in the morning."

It was almost time to leave the office when my phone vibrated on my desk. It was a text from Will.

Will: Chuck, can you go down to St. Mary's hospital? Angus's dad is going in for surgery and Angus is there. I can't go tonight, but someone should.

Me: Of course. What's up with his dad?'

Will: Stomach pains. They found a tumor and he's in surgery right now. Angus is down there with his mom.

Me: I was just leaving work. I'll go straight there.

Will: Thanks, Chuck.

It took me almost an hour to get to St. Mary's, and then finding a parking place took another twenty minutes. The waiting room was crowded when I arrived. Angus and his mom were sitting in a back corner. Janice's eyes were closed, and her head was leaning back against the wall. Angus was leaning forward, his elbows on his knees, studying the carpet.

I touched his shoulder when I reached him, and he looked up. His eyes were red-rimmed, and he looked tired. As soon as he saw me, he stood and pulled me into his arms. "How did you know?"

"Will texted me. Angus, you should have called me."

"You've had a lot going on. I didn't want to bother you."

I pulled back and smacked him in the chest. "Don't be stupid. You know you can always call me. Hi, Janice." She stood and hugged me.

"Thanks for coming, Charlotte."

"Of course." We all sat down, Angus in the middle. "So tell me what's going on."

"Dave's had some pain in his stomach for a while now. He thought it was probably indigestion, so he didn't want to go to the doctor. But this morning, it was hurting so bad he was doubled over, and I finally told him I was calling an ambulance if he didn't let me take him to the doctor. Stubborn man." Janice shook her head. "The doctor sent him to get a CT scan this afternoon. They found a tumor." Her voice broke, and she stopped talking. Angus reached over and took her hand.

"They're doing surgery right now to remove the tumor. They'll biopsy it and hopefully tomorrow we'll know if it's cancer or not."

"I'm so sorry."

"They should have been out of surgery more than an hour ago. We're not sure what's taking so long."

Janice rested her head against the wall again and closed her eyes. I watched the headlines scroll across the muted television mounted on the wall. Angus watched too, but I don't think he was actually reading the captions. His eyes were looking through the television, and I could tell his thoughts were far away.

Almost two hours later, a doctor stepped into the waiting room and looked around. When he found Angus and Janice, he motioned for them to join him in the hall.

"You want to come?" Angus asked.

"That's okay. I'll wait here."

About ten minutes later, Angus walked back into the waiting room. His face was the color of chalk, and his eyes were distant and unfocused. I hurried to meet him. "Angus?" He looked down at me. "Where's your mom?"

"They said she could go into the ICU with him."

"You can go with them, too. You don't have to stay out here with me."

"They'll only let one person at a time back there with him. It should be mom."

"What did they say?"

Angus looked around the crowded waiting room. "Let's go for a walk." I followed him out into the hall, and we walked down several long corridors. Everywhere we went, people were sitting in the scattered seating areas. Finally, we walked through the doors of the hospital to a courtyard outside. Light from the hospital windows made bright, yellow patches on the concrete. No one was out here. I followed Angus to an empty bench, and we sat down. "It's not good," he said.

"What did they say?"

He swallowed hard and leaned forward, putting his head in his hands. "They need to biopsy it, but they could already see where it's spreading, and the doctor is pretty sure it's cancer."

"Oh, Angus, I'm so sorry."

"He hopes we caught it in time so we can treat it, but they won't know for sure where things stand until sometime tomorrow."

I sighed and put my hand on Angus's back. He stiffened at my touch, and then his body started to shake as he cried. I continued rubbing, back and forth, until the shaking stopped, and he relaxed. He leaned on the bench and put his arm around me, pulling me close into his side. "What will Mom do if he doesn't make it?"

"Don't think about that right now. Just have faith he'll make it." I felt Angus nod against my head.

It was a perfect San Francisco night. Above us, a few bright stars bravely fought to be seen over the city lights. A soft breeze gently disturbed the leaves in the trees around us. The air was warm and heavy.

"If you need to go, I understand. You probably had a date tonight."

I shook my head. "The only thing I have tonight is keeping you company. I'm not going anywhere."

Angus sighed and leaned his head against mine. I could tell when he relaxed, because his arm and head felt heavier.

We stayed like that for more than an hour. Angus fell asleep and I let him rest. When his phone rang in his pocket, he jerked awake. He answered his phone, and I pulled out mine. It was almost ten.

"We'll get you something," Angus said into his phone. "Yeah, I am too. Charles is probably hungry, too. I doubt she ate before she came." When he was off the phone, he turned to me. "Dad's sleeping. Mom doesn't want to leave, but she hasn't eaten since breakfast. She's so hungry she's getting shaky. Have you eaten anything?"

I shook my head. "I'll bet you haven't either."

"Not since lunch. Let's go get some sandwiches and bring them back."

When we returned to the hospital, Janice came out to the waiting room, and we ate together. Janice had been crying, but she did her best to sound positive. I watched as each of them tried to make it easier on the other and felt my chest tighten. They were such good people, and I loved them so much. It hurt to see them worrying like this. It also hurt to think of Dave behind the doors of the ICU. I wanted to march back there, tell him a joke, and ruin the punchline. I wanted to hear him tell me I was the worst joke teller he'd ever heard. I wanted him to tease me about being one of the guys, and tell me how surprised he was that one of the boys had turned out so pretty. I wanted him to be okay, so they could all go home together.

Janice went back in with Dave after we ate, and Angus and I prowled the hospital waiting rooms for one that wasn't so crowded. We finally found one in a tucked-away corner. We turned the television to a home remodeling show and watched in silence as a team of workers remodeled a kitchen, and then infomercials started.

We didn't talk. We just sat together on the little couch. "You don't have to stay with me," Angus said sometime after midnight.

"I'll go home when you do, or when your mom comes out of the ICU."

"She probably won't come out unless they kick her out."

"I'm not leaving you out here alone."

He didn't say anything else.

I curled up on one side of the little couch and watched a pressure cooker infomercial until I fell asleep. When I woke up, Angus was asleep on the other end of the couch, his head back against the wall and his legs extended out in front of him. One of his arms was propped on the armrest, the other rested across my ankles.

I freed my legs slowly and deliberately, so I wouldn't awaken him. When I was sure he was still asleep, I ran my fingers through my messy hair, grabbed my purse, and headed to the cafeteria to get us some breakfast.

I called Jayne and took the day off. Dave's biopsy results came back in the afternoon. Dave had cancer. The doctor was optimistic that with one more surgery to remove some cancerous tissue, and aggressive treatment, Dave had a good chance of coming through it. They moved Dave to a recovery room, where he'd stay another night.

Janice, Angus, and I sat in Dave's room talking quietly while Dave slept. A bouquet of flowers arrived from Kyle's family.

"That was so thoughtful of them," Janice said.

I stepped out into the hall and called Kyle.

"Any news?" he asked when he picked up the phone.

"It's cancer. They're cautiously optimistic they'll be able to treat it successfully, but he's got a long road ahead of him."

"Give them our best."

"The flowers are beautiful, Kyle. Thank you."

"Sure. Are you doing okay?"

"I'm tired. I slept in the waiting room last night."

"Do you still want to go to dinner tonight?"

I hesitated. "Can I let you know in an hour or so?" Kyle didn't say anything right away, and I felt compelled to explain. "I don't want to leave if they need me."

Again, there was a pause. "Sure, just let me know when you know."

I put my phone away and looked up to find Angus watching me. He stepped over, put his arm around my shoulders, and started walking toward the front door of the hospital.

"Thanks for staying with me last night, Chuck."

"You're welcome."

"I've got some phone calls to make and a couple of errands to run, so I'll walk you out."

"Are you trying to get rid of me?" I asked.

Angus squeezed my shoulder. "Why would I do that?"

"Fine. I'm going. But I'll be back tomorrow."

"I hope so." Angus squeezed my shoulder, and we each headed to different parking lots.

Chapter 20

I called Kyle when I got to my car.

"Hi." There was a smile in Kyle's voice. "It's only been ten minutes."

"Angus ushered me out the door. I guess they were ready to get rid of me."

"So dinner?"

"Yes, I'm starving."

"Then let's make it an early one."

"I need time to shower, but after that, I can go whenever. Do you mind if we go somewhere quiet? Where we won't get noticed?"

Kyle laughed. "Let's get takeout and eat at home then."

"Is that okay?"

"I don't care where we eat as long as we eat together."

I tried not to grin stupidly.

"Any requests?"

"Surprise me."

I felt like a new person after I'd showered and dressed. I decided to give Kyle a surprise of my own and stopped at La Boudin for a bag of chocolate dipped coconut macaroons. They smelled so good I ate one on the way to Kyle's.

The hall outside Kyle's condo was empty. I'd almost rung the bell before I realized his door was slightly ajar. I pushed it open a little farther, ready to announce myself, when I heard Kyle's voice. I stopped.

"Do you have someone following her?" He sounded angry.

"Of course not. We're lucky Sam broke his arm, or I wouldn't have even been there yesterday." It was Devon. Who was Sam?

"I'm sure your son would be glad to know his accident was good for Dad's business," Kyle said.

I hadn't realized Devon had a son. He was always so focused on the Aldsworths, it was strange to think about him having a life apart from theirs.

"You know what I'm saying, Kyle. Stop acting like I'm the enemy here. I'm trying to help you. And I'm telling you, if you don't get her under control, she's going to ruin you."

"What has she done that's so wrong? She went to the hospital to check on a friend."

"She sat with him for hours. They hugged. She rubbed his back. They slept together on the same couch. All night."

No one spoke for a minute. I could imagine Kyle's face as he imagined the worst.

"How did they sleep together?" I could hear the reluctance in his voice. He wasn't sure if he wanted to know the answer. I almost walked through the door to answer the question myself, but something held me back.

"It's not like they were 'together' together, but Kyle, they were there all night. Just the two of them in that waiting room."

"Except that you were chaperoning them." It made me sick to think he'd been spying on us, watching us sleep.

"Stop acting like a child. I wasn't chaperoning anyone. I

was trying to protect your future. But hey, if I care more about it than you do, tell me. I'll back off and worry only about your dad. You don't have to run for office if you don't want to."

"You know I want to, Devon. And I appreciate you looking out for me, but this feels . . . wrong."

"Look, I can tell Charlotte is a nice girl, but not everyone is cut out for this, and every time we turn around, we're running interference. Doing damage control. And we've only just begun. If you're going to marry her, you've got years, maybe decades of dealing with this, and you've got to get her on board." I rested my head against the door jamb. My stomach was a disastrous jewelry box, the inside a mass of tangled chains.

"They've been friends most of their lives," Kyle said. "He's like her brother, and they . . ." His voice disappeared, and I couldn't hear the rest of what he said.

"That may be true, but if Angela Prescott had been there last night, it wouldn't matter if they were conjoined twins, she'd have managed to make it look like something inappropriate was happening. The fact is, they're not related, and whether they're platonic friends or not doesn't matter if someone wants to twist it and make it look sordid."

"I can't believe you stayed there all night."

"Kyle, I've known your family since before your dad ran for city council. It's my job to look out for you guys. That's what I was doing last night. Protecting you from the malicious rumors you'd have been facing today if the wrong person saw her cozied up to another man." Their voices were getting louder, and I realized they were walking toward the door. I didn't want Kyle to know I'd heard any of this.

I quickly stepped back to the elevator and pushed the button. I let out a deep breath when the door whispered open. I stepped inside but didn't push a button. The door slid quietly shut but didn't move. A minute later, it opened back up, and there stood Kyle and Devon. They looked alarmed when they saw me. Devon recovered first.

"Hi, Charlotte," he said and nodded.

"Hey. How's it going?" I didn't want an answer. I just wanted to sound normal, but my voice sounded strained in my ears.

"Just touching base with Kyle," he said.

"Always strategizing," Kyle sounded as overwrought as I felt, but he'd replaced his surprised look with a smile.

"Remember what I said." Devon stepped onto the elevator as I stepped off. He pushed a button, and then gave us a short salute. "Have a good evening, you two." His eyes didn't leave Kyle's face.

"For someone who was starving, you've hardly touched your food."

I looked down at the cashew chicken and rice I'd been pushing around my plate. "I guess I wasn't as hungry as I thought."

"You want me to take that?" Kyle reached for my plate.

"Sure."

"You hungry enough for a macaroon?" Kyle asked as he walked to the kitchen.

"Sure. I'll take one of those."

The evening's dynamic was all wrong. Kyle was trying to be his usual self, but I knew he had to be thinking about what Devon had said. How could he not? I'd tried to pretend I hadn't heard their conversation, but after a few minutes, I couldn't anymore. All I wanted to do was camp inside my head and process what I'd heard. No, not just what I'd heard. I needed to process everything that had happened over the past few weeks. I'd been so busy trying to make up for what had happened at the benefit, trying to be worthy of a spot in the Aldsworth family, and working to be what Kyle needed me to be, I hadn't thought about what was happening to me. I was wearing myself out with the effort, only to find out today that it wasn't good enough. Would it ever be good enough?

"Maybe we can watch a movie," Kyle said from the kitchen. It sounded like he was rinsing off the dishes. I knew I should go in and help him, but I sat there, numb.

Suddenly I needed air. The walls were closing in around me. My life was closing in around me. I was suffocating in Aldsworth expectations. I pushed myself off the couch and walked out the door off the dining room that led to the balcony.

It wasn't a large balcony, but the view was spectacular. I stood at the rail and watched the early evening sun sparkle on the water between the Golden Gate Bridge and Alcatraz—millions of diamonds catching the light. A breeze lifted my hair, and I turned my face toward it, closing my eyes and letting its gentle fingers sooth my discomfort. For too long now, I'd pushed aside my feelings about what was happening as I attended to what was immediately before me. It was time to pull all those thoughts and feelings out of storage and figure out how to handle them.

"There you are." Kyle came through the door to stand on the balcony with me. He put his arm around my shoulders and leaned on the rail. "Hard to resist this view, isn't it?"

I nodded. I didn't want to talk.

"I love days like this," he continued. "When there's no

fog, you can see all the way to Angel Island."

I nodded again. I probably should have said something, but I didn't want to talk. If I tried to have an everyday conversation, the thoughts and feelings I needed to explore would get piled back into their boxes. I needed them scattered around the floor of my mind, so I could pick them up, sort through them, and decide what to do with them.

"Does a movie sound good?" Kyle asked.

I turned to him and put my arms around his waist. I held him tightly as his arms came around me, one hand smoothing back my hair. I moved one arm up to the back of his head and pulled him toward me until our lips met. He pulled away, a question in his eyes, and I pulled him back again. There was no doubt who was kissing who.

"Does this mean yes to a movie? Or does this mean you have something else in mind?" He was teasing me, but at the moment, I had no sense of humor, no ability to tease or flirt or laugh.

I buried my face in his neck. "It means I need to go home."

Kyle took hold of my shoulders and held me back, studying my face. "Charlotte, is something wrong?"

Yes. Everything is wrong. Every single thing. I still didn't want to talk, but I couldn't leave without a word. "I'm tired."

"Are you okay to drive home?" Why did he have to be so thoughtful and kind?

I nodded and pulled away, but Kyle didn't let go of my hand. We walked through the condo toward the front door. I picked up my purse, and Kyle grabbed his keys off the entry table. He pulled the door shut behind him and then pushed the button to call the elevator. We waited for it to climb to the eleventh floor in silence. I could feel his eyes on me every time he glanced my direction, but I didn't dare look back at him. My mind was a mess, and until I created some order, I didn't know how to behave.

When we reached my car, Kyle held on to my hand, so I couldn't get the key out of my purse. He turned me toward him and put his hands on either side of my neck, his thumbs on my jaw. "Can you tell me what's going on?" My hands moved from his wrists to his elbows and back again.

"Can we talk tomorrow?" My voice felt small.

Kyle nodded against my forehead. "I'll call you in the morning."

I pulled my purse off my shoulder and retrieved the key. I waved at him as I pulled into traffic, but all I felt was sadness.

Chapter 21

*I*t wasn't even eight o'clock when I got home from Kyle's. Mia wasn't home, and I was glad. I needed time to think. I didn't know what time she'd be home, so I quickly changed into pajamas, brushed my teeth, and closed myself in my bedroom. I sat against the headboard and watched the sun slant across my room as it slowly fell from the sky.

I once read a book called *Introduce Yourself to You*. It sounds silly, but I kept thinking about one of the chapters I'd read. It had said the only way to true happiness is to know yourself—your hopes, your desires, your abilities, and your limitations.

I've known my hopes and desires for a long time. One of the biggest has been to find true love, someone to spend my life with. I'm looking for love that lasts forever. I want a passionate love, the kind that inspires love songs and poetry. But I also want a love that brings peace. My parents have that kind of love. No matter what happens, they calm each other and help each other through it. I can remember watching them when I was a teenager. When Grandpa Harris died, Mom just wanted to be with Dad. He held her hand through the funeral arrangements, and when they left the cemetery,

Dad put his arm around Mom, and they walked to the car together. Mom didn't fall apart. She was strong and peaceful because Dad was there.

And it worked both ways. When I was eleven, Dad lost his job. Mom didn't cry or nag or stress. Dad was sitting at the kitchen table when he told her. She turned off the stove and walked over to dad. She stroked the back of his head and told him it was a good thing because now he could find something better. And he did. I knew someday I wanted love like theirs.

A month ago, I thought maybe I'd found it in kind and patient Kyle. When he smiled at me, it felt like the sun was shining, and when he kissed me, I imagined I could write a love song. But I hadn't felt peace for weeks now, and if I married him, I didn't know if I'd ever feel it again.

As the sun disappeared, and my room became dark, I cried. I let myself daydream about what I'd thought was my future with Kyle. In my make-believe life with him, the only public appearances we made were standing behind his father with the rest of the family after an election. We'd cheer at our children's music recitals and basketball games without anyone noticing us. We'd eat at restaurants, and no one would care who we were. We'd plan family vacations and help our children with their homework. We'd live in one house, and it would be beautiful, but cluttered with books, and toys, and paints, and bicycles—all the trappings of an average life.

Missing in my daydream were fundraisers and campaign speeches. There were no second homes on the other side of the country or mean-spirited reporters trying to twist my words to hurt my husband. There were no political strategists, and we didn't need a publicity person spinning everything we did or said. And there were certainly no paparazzi snapping pictures they hoped would ruin our lives.

It was a beautiful daydream. I lay down on my side facing the wall. There, in the glow of the streetlights, was my paper. I'd been so naïve to put a big X through the cons side. There were cons. Very real ones. Big ones. I'd thought if I ignored the cons and concentrated only on the positive, I'd be fine. But putting blinders on had made me unable to see myself. I didn't know myself in this new world. It was time to get reacquainted. I still had the same hopes and desires. I even knew my abilities. It was time to admit my limitations.

Kyle must have been worried about me, because he called at nine o'clock the next morning. "Did I wake you up?" he asked.

"No. I've been up for a while."

"Mom always said it's bad manners to call anyone before nine on a Saturday unless it's an emergency."

"Your mom is a smart woman."

Kyle let out a deep breath. "Can we talk about last night?"

"Yeah. We need to. But not on the phone."

"Have you eaten breakfast?"

"Not yet."

"I can pick up something to eat, and we can go to the Conservatory."

"That sounds nice," I said.

"Can I pick you up in an hour?"

"Sure."

The Conservatory of Flowers is one of my favorite places in the city. Part of Golden Gate State Park, the Conservatory is a giant, Victorian greenhouse that looks like an elaborate birdhouse. The grounds around the greenhouse are colorful, and the air is fragrant. It was a place that had always made me happy, and I was glad Kyle had suggested it.

When we reached the gently sloping hill in front of the greenhouse, Kyle broke out the food he'd brought—raspberry and white chocolate scones, ham and egg muffins, and orange juice. The only thing we talked about as we ate were the flowers spread out in front of us and the food.

Kyle finished eating before me, and when I'd swallowed my last bite, he broached the subject we'd both been carefully avoiding. "What happened last night, Charlotte?"

I pulled my knees up and wrapped my arms around them. I watched a mother scold her little girl for picking a flower, then I took a deep breath and reminded myself what I'd decided sometime in the middle of the night. It was time to share exactly who I was and what I wanted with Kyle.

"First, I want you to know how much you mean to me. You're amazing, and you've been so good to me. I'm glad Jayne introduced us."

"Are you breaking up with me?" Kyle sounded worried.

I started to shake my head and then stopped. "I don't know what I'm doing, Kyle. But I need to tell you some things, and then together we can decide where we go from here." Kyle nodded. "I heard Devon last night."

Kyle groaned. "I never wanted you to hear any of that."

"I know. I didn't want to hear it, either. But I think it was important that I did. It was a wakeup call for me. It forced me to look at what's happening here and figure out what's best for us."

"Charlotte, we're going to be fine. It'll just take some time."

I held up my hand to stop him from continuing. "This isn't easy. I've never been good at sticking up for myself. I

215

think that's why my dating life has always ended up letting me down. But I want to do things right with you. I want us to say what we need to say, and I want us to understand each other. That way no matter what we decide, we can be okay." My voice betrayed me and quavered. Kyle rubbed my back in little circles. It helped calm me, and I continued. "I've fallen in love with you. You're good and kind and everything a girl could want. I knew where I wanted this to go, and I was crossing my fingers it would. But then you told me about your goals, and everything I was picturing for us disappeared."

I smiled. "I'm not good at all this political stuff. If you don't believe me, ask Devon."

"Devon over-reacts. You can't worry about everything he says."

"If you want to be a senator, you have to worry about it, too. The problem is I don't think I'll ever be good at it."

"You'll be fine, Charlotte. It might feel overwhelming right now, but give it time, and it'll become second nature to you."

"I don't think I *want* to be good at it." My voice was quiet. I turned my face a little farther from his so he wouldn't see the tears that slid down my cheeks.

Kyle didn't say anything for a long time. Finally, I interrupted his thoughts. "Kyle, I don't want to spoil your plans. But I wish more than anything in the world you didn't want to follow your dad into politics, because it's a road I can't follow."

There, I'd said what I needed to say. And now all I wanted to do was curl up in a ball and cry. A boulder was pressing down on my chest, and it felt like it might crush me. Kyle's hand moved to my waist, and he pulled me closer to him. I rested my head on his shoulder, and his hand moved up and down my arm.

"I knew this was coming."

"You did?"

"After you left last night, I sat out on the balcony, trying to figure out what had happened. I didn't know you'd heard Devon, so I didn't know what had prompted your disappearing act." We both laughed a little. "I know this has been hard. I don't know how I should have handled it, though. I knew I liked you that first night, but it's not like I could drop this on you on our first date."

"I don't think you handled it wrong. I just wish things were different. I either wish you wanted to live a regular, non-political life, or I wish I could be the wife you need." I laughed, a little louder this time. "Listen to me. I'm talking like you've proposed or something. I'm not trying to put words in your mouth."

"You don't have to. We've both known how we were feeling, and we both know where this has been headed. You weren't wrong."

"Are you sure you want to go into politics?" I cringed. I didn't want to sound like I was issuing an ultimatum. But maybe I was.

"I'm less sure right now than I was yesterday." Kyle turned my face toward his, and we looked at each other for the first time since the conversation had started. "Oh, Charlotte, don't cry." He kissed a tear on each cheek.

"I want you to say you'll forget about politics, but I know if you say that for me, someday you'll probably hate me for it."

"I don't think I could ever hate you."

I felt like I'd swallowed a golf ball, and it had painfully lodged itself in my throat. I swallowed hard and then tried to talk around it, but my voice sounded like someone else. "I don't want to ruin you."

Kyle bristled. "Why would you even say that?"

"I heard Devon."

"Devon doesn't know what he's talking about."

"You know he does. And he's right. I don't know how to do this, and I can't imagine having to guard every word I say and having to be suspicious of everyone I meet. I'm sorry, Kyle."

Kyle leaned back on his elbows, but kept his hand on my back. I was glad. His touch felt like an anchor, holding us in our world—the world I knew was unbearably fragile and was probably about to break into a million pieces.

Minutes passed, and neither of us spoke. I looked across the lawn and flowers. In the distance, a photographer led a bride and groom to a spot behind a wide bed of pink and yellow flowers. The photographer's assistant arranged the bride's long train artistically behind them, and then the photographer began snapping pictures. During the last few shots, the couple kissed.

"Jerks." Kyle caught me off guard, and I laughed. "Seriously, why don't they rub it in our faces?" We laughed.

The entourage moved to the steps in front of the conservatory, not too far from us. Kyle stood and put out his hand to help me up. "This is cruel and unusual punishment. Let's go."

"I think I'm going to Fairfield tomorrow. I need to see my parents," I said on the way back to my apartment.

Kyle laughed. "I was just thinking I needed to have a long talk with Dad and Mom."

I sighed. "Your parents have been so kind to me. I hope they know how much I admire them."

"I'll tell them. Can I come by Monday after work?"

"Of course."

Kyle kissed me goodbye, and for a minute, I wished I could take back everything I'd said. But I knew I couldn't.

Chapter 22

I wasn't sure what I hoped to gain from my visit with my parents. Part of me wanted them to tell me what to do. Whether they said, "Marry him and stop complaining," or "Don't even think of marrying a politician," I'd have been happy to turn over the difficult decision to someone else.

Instead, Dad shook his head. "I don't envy you this one. Not an easy choice."

Mom got tears in her eyes. "There isn't a good option here. Either way you go you lose something."

It felt like a long time before someone spoke. "You've already made your decision, haven't you?" Dad asked.

Tears fell down my cheeks as I nodded. "I can't do it. And it's not just that I'd hate living life like his family has had to, even though I would. It's also because I don't want to ruin things for Kyle, and I would. I'm not good at all of it."

I cried off and on as I told them all that had happened in the last three weeks, including Devon watching me all night at the hospital to be sure I didn't embarrass the Aldsworths. Mom sat by me and held my hand. She cried almost as much as I did.

"I'm so sorry, honey," she said when I was finished. "I

really liked Kyle."

I noticed the way she used the past tense, and even though I knew that was to try to help me as I moved forward, it hurt to think of him as something I was leaving behind. I blew my nose. "I still like him. I love him."

"You're handling this with a lot of maturity," Dad said.

I didn't feel mature. I felt like an angst-filled, weepy teenager.

"Some people never learn that love alone can't make a successful marriage and family," Dad said. "They believe the whole 'love conquers all' thing, and sometimes it doesn't. That's why there are so many divorces. A good marriage takes making a choice with your heart, your head, and your gut, but when you're in the middle of a new romance, it's hard to intelligently use any of those things."

I knew Dad was right. My heart wanted Kyle more than anything, but my head told me the life he was offering wasn't for me, and my gut told me I'd ruin his aspirations.

When it was time to leave, I hugged my parents goodbye. "Maybe after he talks to his parents, he'll decide he doesn't want a life in politics after all," Mom said.

I sighed. "If only."

"What is wrong with you?" Jayne asked when she poked her head into my office the next day.

"You don't know?" I don't know why I figured she'd know. It wasn't like Kyle would have called Trent to discuss our situation.

"Know what?" Jayne's voice was suspicious, and her face already looked pained.

"I don't know if I can talk about this today. Right now

everything's in limbo anyway, so I'm not sure what I'd even say."

"Oh, Charlotte. Are you and Kyle breaking up?"

I swallowed and shrugged my shoulders. I was so tired of crying, and even though my eyes were already red and puffy from the previous forty-eight hours, I didn't want to cry anymore. Especially at work. I needed to laugh. I needed something to lighten the mood. "Hey, at least it won't matter for him since he'll be getting married soon whether it's to me or someone else."

My voice sounded watery in my ears, and my lame attempt at a joke had the opposite effect on my state of mind. I reached for a Kleenex.

"That's not funny, Charlotte. I know I joked about that, but I wanted things to work out for you two. I promise I wasn't using you as a sacrificial lamb."

"I know. Don't you dare start crying, Jayne. I'm trying to hold it together, and I don't want to see you mourning us before anything is even official.

"I thought things were going so well."

"They were. They were perfect," I said.

"Then what's the—"

"Please don't," I interrupted. "I can't do this right now."

"Okay. Just remember I'm here whenever you want to talk," Jayne said from the doorway.

"I know. Thank you."

"Don't thank me. I feel terrible. I never wanted you to get hurt in all this."

"Jayne?" She turned to look at me. "I'm not sorry you set us up, even if it doesn't work. Kyle is even better than you said he was."

Jayne shook her head. "I know you don't want to talk about it. That's fine. I'm just so confused."

I took great care to look as nice as I could. I wore jeans and a lacy, white blouse. I'd managed to keep the tears in check throughout the day, so my eyes looked almost normal. When Mia heard Kyle was coming by, she took off to the movies with a friend.

Ever since I'd left my parents the evening before, I'd been daydreaming about what would happen when Kyle came over tonight. It was perfectly laid out in my mind. Kyle would knock on the door, and I'd open it wide. He'd smile at me and take me in his arms. After holding me close for a few minutes, he'd say, "Let's sit down. I need to tell you my decision." We'd sit on the couch together, and Kyle would play with my hair and touch my cheek. He'd tell me he'd done a lot of soul-searching the last couple of days, and he knew there were some things he could live without. He could live without fame and fortune and a political future. But the one thing he couldn't live without was me. He'd talked to his parents, and they'd given their blessing to us getting married and Kyle working for the rest of his career in the family business. Then he'd kiss me senseless and pull out a small box that held the symbol of everything I'd hoped for.

It was a perfect daydream, and I'd almost started to believe it was a possibility.

I was ready for my daydream to come true when I opened the door. What I wasn't ready for was the sad smile of defeat. I swallowed a sob. Kyle's eyes were red-rimmed and tired. He was wilted and forlorn.

"Oh, Kyle." I sagged against the door. He stepped inside and sat down on the edge of the couch. He looked tense and ready to make a quick escape. My daydreams had not prepared me for reality. I forced myself to breathe. I sat down beside him and put my hand through his arm, until it clasped his hand. I was glad when he held mine back and closed his other hand over it.

"You go first," I said softly.

His Adam's apple moved up and down his throat as he swallowed hard. I waited while he found his words. Finally, his eyes focused on my hand in his, and he started. "My parents think you're pretty amazing."

"I'll bet they do." It was difficult to keep the sarcasm from my voice.

"They do. Mom was sad because she thinks you're great. Dad said it takes a pretty remarkable girl to put someone else's needs first." A tear dropped onto my arm, and I realized Kyle was crying. I snuggled into his side and rested my head on his shoulder. "I wish I could turn my back on it all, but I can't. There are twenty years of expectations on my shoulders. And I know I can do good for people. I've had every possible advantage, and I can't turn my back on the obligation I've always felt that I have to contribute something."

I nodded. I understood how he felt. I was just so disappointed.

"I wish I could change things," Kyle continued. "I wish I didn't feel like I had to do this, or that you could be excited about it with me."

I didn't know what to say. I'd never felt such crushing sadness at a breakup before. In the past, one or both of us had not felt enough for the other. This was different. Kyle and I loved each other. But every time I tried to pep talk myself into believing love would get us through this, I thought of Angela Prescott twisting my words. I thought of someone using me as a tool to destroy the good Kyle could do, and I knew no matter how much we loved each other, I would never be the right choice for the life he felt he had to live.

"It's funny," Kyle said. "You're the best woman I've ever dated. You're so genuine and open, and I love that about you. But I also know those are the things that make this too much for you."

"My dad reminded me last night that successful marriages are made by people who go into them paying attention to their heart, their mind, and their gut. I'm trying to do that, even though it's killing me."

Kyle nodded. "See, that's why you'd be such a good wife."

"But so horrible at politics."

"I'm not going to try to change your mind." Kyle fidgeted with my fingers. "Even though I want to more than anything."

"And I'm not going to try to change yours, even though I wish I could."

Kyle sat back on the couch and reached out, pulling me snugly against him. We laced our fingers together across our laps and sat there silently for a long time.

"This is certainly different than any breakup I've ever been through," Kyle said, and we laughed a little.

"Me too."

"I feel like we'd make it easier on each other if we found something to argue about. We could yell and scream, and you could slam the door as I left. Then you could tell all your friends what a jerk I am."

"And you could tell all yours you don't know what you ever saw in me."

"Then everyone would start setting us up again, so we could get each other out of our systems, and we'd be happy to move on."

"What do you want to argue about?" I asked. Kyle lifted one corner of his mouth.

"I don't want to argue. I just want to sit here and memorize everything about you so tomorrow or next week, when I'm missing you, I can wallow in the sad memory of it all."

"What will you remember?" I asked, knowing I was torturing us both, but also knowing I wanted to wallow in some of the pain together.

"This little freckle right here." Kyle tapped a freckle on my hand with his thumb. "I first noticed it when we were making cheese."

"You did not."

"I did too. Don't question my memories, Charlotte."

I giggled. "Okay. I apologize."

"I'm going to miss the smell of your hair." He breathed in my hair. "You have the best-smelling hair I've ever dated."

I laughed. "Speaking of hair, yours is ridiculous. You have to go into politics just because of that hair." I pulled my hand from his long enough to tousle his soft hair. "And I'm going to miss your manners. You're such a gentleman."

"I'm going to miss your wakeboarding."

I punched him. "You won't miss that at all."

"I actually will. I'll never be able to wakeboard again without thinking of you."

"It'll give you a good laugh, that's for sure." Kyle's hand was making circles on my arm, and I didn't ever want them to end.

"I won't laugh when I think about it. I'll think about how hard you tried and what a good sport you were, even when you were waterlogged and embarrassed. Man, you were cute."

"You know you'll laugh. You don't have to sugarcoat it for me." Kyle laughed. "See, you're laughing about it right now."

"You're right. I'll probably laugh."

We fell silent for a few minutes. "Your smile," I said.

"What?"

"I love your smile. I'm going to miss it."

"Speaking of mouths," Kyle said.

"I didn't say mouth. I said smile. That includes your eyes, you know."

"That's great. But I want to talk about your mouth. I'm going to miss a lot more about your mouth than just your smile." He was killing me. And then he touched my lips with his finger. "I'm going to miss everything about your mouth."

I took hold of his wrist, held his fingers to my lips, and kissed them. And then Kyle leaned over and kissed me. It was long and slow and unbearably sad. Neither of us wanted it to end. When it did, we'd never feel each other's lips again. So we made it last. Kyle put his arms around my shoulders and held me there. I let my fingers run through his hair. When our tears mingled together, I pulled away and bit my quivering lip.

Kyle stood and pulled me to my feet. We walked to the door, holding hands.

"I love you," I said. Kyle pulled me into his arms and held me tightly against him.

"I love you, too." I wanted to kiss him again, so much I ached clear to my toes, but I think we both knew if we started kissing again, we wouldn't be able to say goodbye.

When Kyle left, I watched him all the way down the stairs. He looked up and our eyes held for a moment. After he went through the door, I hurried over to the window and watched him out on the sidewalk. Cuddy was there, and I watched the two men talk for a minute. Kyle looked up and winked at me. After a minute, he started down the sidewalk. His car was about halfway down the block. He looked back at me over the top of his car.

I hoped he couldn't see the tears streaming down my cheeks. Even though it was probably the corniest thing I'd ever done, I blew Kyle a kiss. He smiled and blew one back. Then he got in his car and left.

Chapter 23

I didn't call Angus for therapy. In the past, therapy had always been a rite of passage, symbolically preparing me to move on.

I was nowhere close to being ready to move on. Even though Angus was a pro at telling me what I needed to hear, I didn't want to hear any of it. I couldn't bear the thought of anyone telling me there were other fish in the sea, or there was someone even better out there for me. I hoped it was true, but right now I couldn't imagine it. I needed to mourn what I'd had with Kyle.

Strangely, I not only needed to mourn. I wanted to mourn. I wanted to remember how good Kyle was and how good he'd been to me. He'd made every other relationship feel like they'd happened to a child. Kyle had been a grown up love, a plan for the future love, and a put each other first love.

I'd never had that before. I'd never willingly broken my heart for someone else, and the more I thought about it, the more I realized Kyle had done the same for me. He hadn't tried to pressure me or make me change my mind. He hadn't asked me to do something I wasn't capable of doing. We'd both given up what we'd wanted to make the other one happy. That made the loss both easier and more difficult, and I couldn't voice these things to anyone else. Voicing it would undermine the love and pain and sacrifice.

Jayne hugged me when she saw me and offered to talk whenever I was ready. I nodded, but knew it would be a while. Dad and Mom called to check on me, but didn't ask for any specifics. They just reminded me they loved me. Mia offered silent support, never asking me any questions. She just tried to keep me occupied.

It had been three weeks since I'd seen Kyle, when my phone chirped. It was Angus.

Angus: You up for some therapy?

I panicked. Had someone told him about Kyle and me? I didn't need to ask him because the phone chirped again.

Angus: I guess we need to make sure Kyle's okay with us having therapy.

It was then I realized he wasn't talking about my breakup. He must have split with Wyatt.

Me: Of course we can go to therapy. I'm so sorry, Angus. Are you doing okay?

Angus: I'll be fine. It's always a little hard, even when you know it's not a permanent thing.

Me: When do you want to go?

Angus: Is tonight too short of notice?

Me: No. Tonight's great. You want to meet there?

Angus: I can swing by and pick you up. No sense having two cars to park.

Me: Sounds good.

Angus: Eight?

Me: I'll be ready.

I felt a little guilty. I'd have to tell Angus about Kyle tonight. I hoped when I did, he wouldn't feel betrayed that I hadn't followed our usual pattern. Hopefully, he'd understand. It would be good to see him. I felt a stab of pain as I realized that within a matter of weeks, I'd lost Kyle forever, and I'd lose Angus to his residency back east.

I took a deep breath and let it out slowly. I reminded myself I had a great job and good friends. I just needed to be patient while I waited for true love.

No. I'd had that. Now I was waiting for a love that would work.

Angus double parked and called my cell phone. "I'm here."

I noticed the sharp contrast between Kyle's ridiculously nice car and medical student, Angus's, fourteen-year-old Toyota Camry.

"How's your dad doing?" I asked.

"Pretty good. He's started treatment. It's been miserable, but he's determined to beat this. He says he wants to be around for me to operate on his knees, and he'd like to meet his daughter-in-law and grandchildren before he goes."

"Your dad is such a great man. If anyone can get through this, it'd be him. How did your parents take your breakup?"

"I don't know. They liked Wyatt."

"I liked her, too. I thought you were a good match."

"She was great. There just wasn't that thing, you know? I never felt more than friendship. I wanted to, but I didn't."

"What about Wyatt? Is she okay?"

"She cried. I felt like a jerk, but I never led her on. She said all along she was good with the 'just friends' thing. I guess she was saying what she thought I wanted to hear."

"Why do relationships have to be so hard?" I whispered.

"I don't think they are hard when you find the right one. At least that's what Will keeps telling me."

"I'm not sure you can use Will and Gina as a measuring stick. They knew they wanted to marry each other the first night they met. And I don't think they've had a disagreement yet."

"So maybe he does know what he's talking about."

We sat in a back booth and ordered our usual. After the waitress left, Angus relaxed into the corner of the booth and put one leg up on the bench.

"When do you leave for New York?" I asked, even though the thought of it made me lonely.

"Well, the New York residency started last week."

"Really? Did they give you a little extra time because of your dad?"

Angus shook his head. "Nope. I actually went in and spoke to the Chief of Staff at Alameda, and I'm staying here."

"You are?" A small strand of the rope that had been strangling my heart loosened.

"I couldn't stand the thought of being so far from Dad.

They were hours away from giving the spot to someone else, but after I talked to him, he said I could take it. So I'm staying."

"I'll bet your parents were so happy."

"Yeah, they were. I was excited to see a new part of the country, but I feel good about it."

"So do I." We smiled at each other. "I hated the thought of you being so far away."

"Well, you're all stuck with me for several more years. Unless you marry the future senator and you move back east. I keep watching for a gigantic ring."

I took a long drink of water. "We're not actually dating anymore."

"What?" Angus turned in his seat and leaned across the table. "What are you talking about? Since when?"

"Three weeks ago. I'm sorry I didn't tell you. I just . . ."

Angus put up his hand. "You don't have to be sorry. I get it."

"You do?"

"I know this one was different. If you aren't ready to talk about it, I understand."

I nodded. "This has been so hard," I whispered as tears started flowing again.

"Oh, Charles." Angus slid out from his side of the booth and scooted in by me. He put his arm around me and smoothed my hair, while I cried into his shoulder. "I thought this was it for you."

"So did I." I sniffled.

"What happened?"

"It was all very mature and rational. And sad. I can't live with that kind of scrutiny and mistrust. Not mistrust from Kyle," I quickly explained.

"I know what you mean. That reporter messed with your head."

I nodded. "And fear. I was so afraid I'd do or say something wrong. I knew I'd ruin things for him."

"No, you wouldn't have. He'd have been lucky to have you on his team."

"I'd have been lucky to have him, Angus. And yes, I would have ruined things for him. I learned some things about myself. I hadn't realized I'm such a private person. I don't want everyone watching my every move, and I don't want to have to be on guard about every word that comes out of my mouth. I'd already made some big mistakes."

"I don't believe that."

"It's true. It was a mutual decision. But it's been hard." I didn't tell him about the last straw—Devon watching me overnight because he didn't trust that I wasn't cheating or doing something that would embarrass the Aldsworths. I'd said enough. "I think I'm done for a while."

"Done with what?"

"Dating. I've always been afraid to turn anyone down because what if I'm rejecting 'the one?'"

"You turned down Eldon Wentworth."

"You can't count that. I knew there was no way he was the one. He spit when he talked, and he couldn't say a word to me without being this close." I put my face right next to Angus's to prove my point. "Besides, when he asked me to dinner, I couldn't go. That was the same night as McKayla's graduation."

Angus moved his face back a little bit. "I don't know, Chuck. He might have been 'the one.'"

"If he was, I'm better off single the rest of my life."

"I've suggested setting you up with Charlie three or four times, and you've turned me down on that."

"His name is Charlie."

Angus shook his head. "He's a good guy. You might be

missing out on 'the one.' Maybe you should let me set you up. You might hit it off."

"Thanks anyway, but I won't be ready to date for a long time. This one hurt too much."

"Let me know if you change your mind. He lives in Sacramento. You could meet in the middle. Or you could go out some time when you go see your parents."

Suddenly, I felt very selfish. "No more talking about me, Angus. This was supposed to be your therapy session." I wanted to lighten the mood and talk about something else.

"It seems like we both needed it."

"Thanks for understanding why I hadn't said anything. And thanks for taking the Alameda position. I'm glad you're not leaving."

"Me too."

Our meal came, and we ate too much. I laughed for the first time in three weeks. It was after ten when we walked to Angus's car.

"So, how long do you think it'll take Kyle to marry someone else?" I asked. It was something I'd thought about a lot the last three weeks, and the thought hurt my heart.

"Stop it, Chuck. Don't even think about that. It's all just stupid coincidence, anyway."

I knew better, but I didn't want Angus to have to pep talk me anymore. "I was just wondering."

Chapter 24

Six Months Later

I 'd been to Imperial Palace a few times with Aleena. The food was legendary, but taking someone who could speak Mandarin was the only way to survive the place. Imperial Palace was in San Francisco's Chinatown, but once you walked through the doors, you might as well have been in Shanghai. The restaurant had been a dance hall in the 1940s. Seventy years ago the entrance had been through double doors at the back of the room, but now we entered onto what had once been the stage where bands performed. Eight steps led down to what had been the dance floor, but was now filled with round tables with yellow tablecloths. A dozen chandeliers hung overhead, the most obvious remnant of its fancy past life.

Long walkways looked like mazes. Between the walkways were clusters of tables squeezed together so tightly, it was difficult to distinguish the different groups of diners. We followed a tiny Chinese woman to a table in the middle, carefully dodging the carts of food being pushed around by a host of Chinese servers. Imperial Palace was probably the loudest restaurant in the city. Servers yelled at the diners, and diners yelled back their orders. Table conversations were carried out with raised voices. I wasn't sure which would have registered a higher decibel level—a world cup soccer match or Imperial Palace on a Friday afternoon.

I looked around the crowded room. I'd only seen one other non-Asian at the restaurant in all the times I'd eaten there, and that had been during our second lunch. It had been an older white man with a group of Chinese friends. Today, I was the only non-Asian in the room.

We'd been seated all of four seconds when the first cart bumped into the back of Aleena's chair and a woman began screaming at her. I grinned. I couldn't help it. This place was an adventure.

"You want pork buns?" Aleena yelled at me.

"Yes. And purple rice," I yelled back.

For the next few minutes, Aleena yelled and argued with the servers pushing the carts. When they wanted to give us something we hadn't asked for, she shook her head and yelled at them. When they passed us without offering something we wanted, Aleena hollered at them for their negligence. About five minutes later, we had everything we wanted on the table, and we began eating.

There was a break in the clamor and I looked around. All over the room, diners had turned their attention toward the entrance. I followed their eyes, and suddenly I understood the hush.

"Look at those brave men." Aleena was looking the same place I was.

Standing inside the doors were two men who were as out of place as Mike Tyson on a synchronized swim team. I stared at them along with the rest of the room as they waited to be seated. It was hard to drag my eyes away. Not only were they unusually tall, they were also two of the most handsome men I'd seen in some time.

"Do the Hemsworths have two brothers we don't know about?" I asked.

Aleena giggled. "Apparently."

Although the men bore a striking resemblance to our favorite Australian imports, they each had their own vibe. One was clean-shaven and polished and wore a tailored, navy suit, while the other wore faded jeans, a plaid shirt with the sleeves rolled up to the elbows, and a few day's scruff. He reminded me of a lumberjack, and it wasn't hard to picture his broad shoulders and muscular forearms felling giant redwoods.

I couldn't help laughing as the less-than-five-foot Chinese woman barked orders for the two big men to follow her. She walked straight to the table next to ours. "You sit here," she yelled and pointed at the table. They obeyed.

When she turned to leave, they both started laughing. "Well, she's a bit cranky," the lumberjack said. His English was laden with an accent I couldn't place.

Around us, the noise picked back up, but I barely noticed. The table where they sat was practically on top of ours. In fact, the man in the suit was sitting so close to me that with only a minor adjustment, we'd be rubbing shoulders. The lumberjack was sitting nearly as close to Aleena, which gave me a perfect angle to look at him. He had a captivating face. His complexion was ruddy, like he sported a little sunburn. A smattering of freckles crossed his cheekbones and nose. His hair was the color of sweet

238

potatoes and made the blue of his eyes startling.

Two women pushed a cart up to the table and began yelling in Mandarin. The men looked at each other. "What do we do?" the suited man yelled and his friend shrugged.

As if in response to his question, the women started holding up plates of food while shouting and pointing. The two men looked at each other and then back at the women. "Do you speak English?" the lumberjack asked.

"No, no." One of the Chinese women shoved a plate of noodles toward them.

"You want these?" the suited man asked his companion.

"I dunno what I want. I'm thinkin' this was a mistake."

I couldn't help but laugh at their discomfort. "Do you need some help?" I hollered. Both men turned to look at me.

"Aye, we do, miss. But you don't fit in here anymore than we do," the man in the suit shouted.

"But I brought my secret weapon." I pointed at Aleena, who grinned at the men and waved.

"Can ya help us out?" asked the man in the plaid shirt.

"Sure." Aleena slid around to the seat beside mine, and we moved our food to our side of the table. "You should join us over here."

The men moved to the other side of our table. The Chinese women at the cart shook their heads and pushed the cart over to our table. Within a few minutes, they had several dishes in front of them, and Aleena had successfully shooed the servers away.

"We asked where we could get the best Chinese food in town and this is where they sent us. I was thinkin' we might need to go and find a piece instead." The lumberjack took a large bite of pork roll. "This is good."

"A piece?" I asked, trying to make sense of what he'd said.

"He means a sandwich," said the suited man. "I'm Bruce, by the way, and this is my brother, Flynn."

Flynn swallowed and nodded, "Nice ta meet ya."

"Where are you from?" I asked.

"Stornaway, on the Isle of Lewis."

I must have looked confused because Bruce spoke up. "Scotland."

"Aye, aye," I said and then felt foolish. Did they even say "aye aye" in Scotland? When I looked up, Flynn was grinning at me. My stomach did a little dip I hadn't felt for months. I couldn't help but smile back. In fact, we sat frozen like that for several seconds before I started feeling silly and pulled my eyes away from his.

It was hard to carry on a conversation in the commotion of Imperial Palace. We tried, but we kept having to repeat ourselves, so mostly we ate and laughed at the chaos around us. I found myself glancing at Flynn throughout the meal and he was almost always looking back at me. My stomach was a flurry of activity. A waiter came to the table and began adding up the cost of each of the plates of food. We tried to separate the dishes so we could each pay for our own, but in the end, the waiter handed us one bill. Bruce put up his hand and brushed Aleena's away. "No worries. We'll cover it."

"Oh no, we can get ours."

"Ya helped us out. We'll buy your lunch."

The street sounded almost like the inside of a church after the noise of the restaurant. We stopped on the sidewalk and turned to thank our new Scottish friends.

"Thanks for the help. We mighta starved without ya." Flynn winked at me. What was it about his appearance that made it hard to look away? Certainly he was handsome, but I came in contact with attractive men regularly and they didn't

240

make me want to gawk at them. There was just something about his pale blue eyes and the scattered freckles that made me think of explorers and pioneers and Vikings. He was so manly.

"You two are brave. I wouldn't dare come here without Aleena," I said.

"What brings you to the U.S?" I was glad Aleena had asked. I'd wanted to know but had been too busy staring to speak.

"'I've lived here almost two years. Flynn's a tourist. Just got here yesterday."

"Visiting your fair country for a while. Likin' the sights so far." Flynn nodded at me.

My cheeks grew warm.

"There's a lot to see here. Are you playing tour guide?" Aleena asked Bruce.

"When I have the time. There's a lot I still haven't seen. I've been here two years and haven't made it to Alcatraz."

"Be sure to do that while he's here," Aleena said.

"And Musee Mechanique." I'd finally found my voice.

"Hawl?" Flynn said.

"What?" I asked.

"Sorry," Bruce interjected. "Hawl means excuse me. I think he was asking you what you said. Music what?"

We all laughed. "I thought English was Scotland's official language," I said.

"Aye, it is, but it's a bit different."

"I said Musee Mechanique. It's a game emporium down on the wharf. The owner has been collecting carnival-type games for decades. There are some great ones in there. Be sure to go there."

"Thanks for the tip," Bruce said. "Sadly I have ta work while he's here, so he has to play tourist on his own much of the time."

"Where do you work?" Aleena asked.

"Bryant and Schullman. I'm an architect there."

My phone vibrated in my pocket. It was Jayne.

Jayne: You coming back to the office today?

Me: I'll be there in twenty minutes. Everything okay?

Jayne: Stop by and see me when you get back.

"It looks like I'm being summoned back to the office." I slipped my phone back in my pocket.

"It was grand meetin' ya." Flynn shook Aleena's hand and then mine.

"Enjoy your stay." I pulled my hand away and took a step back. Sure Flynn was wildly interesting and I sorta wanted to count his freckles, but I wasn't interested in men right now. And I certainly wasn't going to break my dating fast on a tourist who'd be leaving the country in a few days. I slowly backed away until Aleena finally got the hint and waved goodbye.

"What was the rush?"

"No rush. I've got to get back to work."

"Uh huh." Aleena looked disgusted.

"What? I have a job, you know."

"And that was all about the job. A gorgeous guy can't take his eyes off you and looks like he might ask you out, and you've got to get back to work."

"I'm not dating right now."

"Charlotte, it's been six months."

"Your point?"

Aleena groaned. "My point is that you've avoided guys long enough. Maybe it's time to move on."

"I'm not ready yet. Besides, he's visiting. He won't even be here that long."

Aleena shrugged. "Sounds perfect to me. Good looking guy. Great accent. No pressure. Perfect situation to ease you back into dating. A no-stress rebound guy. Think about it."

I shook my head. "So you're saying I should use him?"

"That sounds so harsh. It could be mutually beneficial. You use him to help you ease back into dating and he uses you as a tour guide. It sounds like a win win."

We reached my car. "Maybe you should date him."

"I'm not the one he kept looking at." Aleena hugged me. "Thanks for lunch."

I walked straight to Jayne's office when I got back to work. When she heard me, Jayne looked up. Her face scared me. Had someone died? "Jayne, what's wrong?"

"Oh Charlotte." Tears sprang into Jayne's eyes. She leaned back in her chair and covered her mouth. Her eyes were tortured.

"Jayne, are you okay?" She shook her head in response. I sat in a chair across the desk from her and leaned forward. "Tell me what's wrong."

"Kyle's engaged."

I collapsed back in the chair, my legs splayed at odd angles. Thoughts and emotions exploded and faded like a fireworks display. Shock flashed red and died away. Envy blasted green and fell at my feet. Searing disappointment burst through my heart and then slowly paled to a dull ache.

Of course he was. What did I expect? Why would Kyle be any different than anyone else?

"I feel so bad that I ever joked about this with you? I

didn't want him to marry anyone but you. I kept thinking you two would work it out. I'm so sorry."

I pulled myself out of my chair and Jayne hurried around the desk. "Don't feel bad," I managed as she hugged me.

"But I do."

I shook my head. "Don't. It's okay." I pulled away and stepped to the doorway. "Kyle deserves to be happy." I turned away. I couldn't risk Jayne's tears melting me into a puddle.

Kyle was getting married. I should have asked Jayne who he was marrying, but I didn't really want to know.

Who was I kidding? Of course I wanted to know. Was she pretty? Did she come from a political family? How old was she?

As soon as I got to my office, I pulled up google and typed: Kyle Aldsworth engaged. Then I clicked on images.

I almost choked. The first picture that came up was Kyle and me, walking out of the Mercy House benefit. That was a bit of cruel irony.

Then I saw the second picture.

Of course.

Note from Karey White

I hope you enjoyed The Husband Maker and Charlotte's search for a husband of her own. I hope you'll join us for The Matchmaker, book 2 in The Husband Maker Series, as Charlotte continues her quest for her own happily ever after.

If you enjoyed The Husband Maker, I'd be grateful if you'd leave a review on Goodreads, Amazon, or wherever else you review books.

Be sure to sign up for my newsletter for updates and information regarding new releases at kareywhite.com.

Coming Next in
The
Husband Maker
Series

Acknowledgements

When I wrote my first book, I was teased by a reviewer for the long list of people I thanked. She said I thanked everyone but my dog. How sad that I left our old Great Dane off the list. She sits by my feet as I write. I'm sorry, Pepper, for the oversight.

There are many people I need to thank for their support and contributions to this book. Thank you to my first readers, Mom and Dad, Lori, and Savannah (boy did I miss you, Veronica). Thanks for your feedback and for always asking for more. Thank you to Leslie, Rachael, Kaylee, Kathy, Corinne, and Stephanie for your valuable input. Your suggestions made the book better. Thank you Lisa for getting medical school/residency answers for me and thank you Brian for providing me with job information.

Thank you to Leslie for shooting great covers for this series and to Rachael for your design help. Thank you to the cooperative and attractive models—Bruce, CJ, Connor, Hannah, Harrison, Michaela, Skyler, Taz, and Will. Thanks Tricia, for your help & brownies.

Thank you Rachael for brainstorming sessions and for teaching me how to format and typeset.

Thank you Kathy for your help with marketing & publicity.

Most of all, thank you to my family—my husband and kids who put up with me being on the computer too many hours, who repeat themselves if I missed what they said because I was plotting in my mind, who pitch in around the house, and who offer love and words of encouragement.

I am very blessed.

About the Author

*K*arey grew up in Idaho, Oregon, Missouri and Utah. Through the years, she's been a student, a teacher, a secretary, a clothing designer and seamstress, a wedding cake maker, a crafter, a scrapbooker, a cook, a housekeeper (alright, this skill she's still working on) a homework helper (until they pass her in math, somewhere around the third grade), and a calm and ladylike fan at her children's sporting events.

Nothing makes her happier than being with family and friends, eating good food and sharing good conversation and a few laughs. When she's with witty and clever people, she could stay there for hours. She loves to travel and see new places. Someday she hopes to take research trips to Norway, Iceland, Scotland, Denmark (while the tulips are in bloom), China, and New Zealand.

She and her husband are the parents of four children that make them look good. She loves salmon and marzipan (not necessarily together) and getting letters. Find out more about Karey and her books at kareywhite.com

If you enjoyed *The Husband Maker,* check out *Prejudice Meets Pride* by Rachael Anderson.

After years of pinching pennies and struggling to get through art school, Emma Makie's hard work finally pays off with the offer of a dream job. But when tragedy strikes, she has no choice but to make a cross-country move to Colorado Springs to take temporary custody of her two nieces. She has no money, no job prospects, and no idea how to be a mother to two little girls, but she isn't about to let that stop her. Nor is she about to accept the help of Kevin Grantham, her handsome neighbor, who seems to think she's incapable of doing anything on her own.

Prejudice Meets Pride is the story of a guy who thinks he has it all figured out and a girl who isn't afraid to show him that he doesn't. It's about learning what it means to trust, figuring out how to give and to take, and realizing that not everyone gets to pick the person they fall in love with. Sometimes, love picks them.

www.ingramcontent.com/pod-product-compliance
Lightning Source LLC
Chambersburg PA
CBHW060421180626
46817CB00007B/2604